BELPHEGOR
THE PHANTOM OF THE LOUVRE

Scorpionic

BELPHEGOR
THE PHANTOM OF THE LOUVRE
Arthur Bernede
ISBN 978-1-902197-53-1
A Scorpionic Book
Published 2012 by Creation Oneiros
Copyright © Creation Publishing

CONTENTS

PART ONE

CHAPTER I
THE ROOM OF THE BARBAROUS GODS

There is a ghost at the Louvre!

Such was the strange rumour which, on the morning of the 17th May, 1925, was circulated in our national picture gallery.

Everywhere – in the vestibules, in the passages, the staircases – one saw only people gathered together: frightened and incredulous, feverishly speculating on the strange and fantastic news.

In the Room of the Barbarous Gods, in front of the the celebrated painting "The Metamorphosis of Lucifer", two guards were talking animatedly about the macabre story.

Shortly, the cleaners – who, on this day, only did their work in a distracted manner – approached them in order to listen avidly to their conversation.

"I tell you that it must be a ghost," said one of the guards. The other man burst out laughing, and shrugged his shoulders. "Gautrais has seen it! And he is not joker or a coward! He went to report it to the curator."

In the office of this high official, Pierre Gautrais, a gallant, robust fellow with square shoulders and an honest face, reported the incident to his superior, M. Lavergne, who sat in front of his desk with his colleague and secretary and listened to him in a friendly but rather sceptical manner.

"I have seen him as I see you now! I would cut off my head rather than deny it."

"Tell me, Gautrais, you had not been drinking a little too much?" observed M. Lavergne.

'Oh, no sir, you know quite well that I never get drunk."

"Then it was a hallucination, perhaps?'

"Oh, no sir. I was very much awake – quite in control of

myself."

"At what time did this phenomenon show itself?" asked the assistant-curator.

"One o'clock in the morning, M. Rabusson," replied the guard. "I was just making my round in the rooms on the ground floor which look out on to the water, when – all of a sudden – on arriving in the Room of the Barbarous Gods, I saw a human form who, robed in a black shroud and wearing a kind of hood, turned its back on me and went and stood close to the statue of Belphegor.

"Seizing my revolver, I shot in its direction. I saw it at the moment where, after mounting the steps, it reached the landing and, levelling my weapon at it, I shouted, 'Halt or I shall shoot!' But scarcely had I put my finger to the trigger than the phantom made a jump sideways and disappeared as if it had melted into the darkness."

Visibly impressed by the sincerity of the guard, whom everyone highly respected, M. Lavergne looked from one to the other of his colleagues, who appeared scarcely less perplexed than he by the story which they had just heard.

Then, getting up, he said: "Ah, well! We are going to see; follow me, Gautrais."

They soon reached the Room of the Barbarous Gods, where a group of employees were talking in front of the statue of the arch-demon, Belphegor. As soon as they saw the new arrivals, they hurriedly moved away, with the exception of the chief guard, Jean Sabarat, a well-built, athletic figure of a man. Respectfully taking off his cap, Sabarat turned towards the curator and said: "Sir, some traces have been discovered over here."

M. Lavergne approached and examined the statue closely. He saw some quite deep scratches, which looked as though they had just been done and which appeared to have been made with the aid of a cold chisel.

Troubled by this discovery, the curator said: "This seems highly unusual. Is it possible that a burglar has broken into the building?"

M. Lavergne decided that he would inform the police. He went away with his colleagues, but Sabarat, an idea suddenly coming to him, ran after them and said: "Sir, if we bring the police into this affair, the ghost – or whatever it is – will take care not to reappear."

"Quite true."

"I ask your permission to hide myself tonight in this room... and I guarantee that if our phantom appears again, I will deal with him."

"What do you think of it, gentlemen?" asked M. Lavergne.

"Sabarat makes sense," said M. Rabusson.

"Very well! It is agreed, my good Sabarat – tonight you shall be on guard!"

All three left the room.

As soon as they had disappeared, Gautrais went up to Sabarat and said to him: "Sir, would you like me to stay with you here on tonight?"

"Thank you, my good man, but there's no need!"

And so, still not able to shake the events of the preceding night from his mind, Gautrais rejoined his wife, who was awaiting for him anxiously in the courtyard of the Louvre.

"Any news?" she asked.

In a sombre voice, Gautrais replied: "Nothing, Marie-Jeanne! That is to say, yes – Sabarat has asked permission to stay tonight all alone in the Room of the Barbarous Gods. I wished to stand guard with him... but he will not let me."

"I am very glad."

"Why?"

"Because I have a feeling that anyone who mixes themselves up in this affair will meet with misfortune."

"Come now, you talk nonsense."

"We shall see. My presentiments are always right."

Madame Gautrais was indeed correct. The passing of the vigil transformed itself into one of the most mysterious and frightening dramas which had ever been known at the museum.

The next day Gautrais, who had not closed his eyes since one o'clock, was the first to enter the Room of the Barbarous Gods; there he discovered, close by the statue of Belphegor, the inanimate body of Sabarat.

Stifling an anguished cry, Gautrais bent over his fallen comrade. Although the body of the chief guard showed no signs of any wound, it also gave no sign of life. His revolver lay in his shrivelled clutch.

Mad with fright, Gautrais ran into the next gallery and called in a thunderous voice: "Help! Help!"

On hearing his cry, two guards rushed in and gathered round Sabarat who, his eyes closed, was breathing very faintly.

"Alive! He's still alive!" exclaimed Gautrais.

One of his colleagues, who had just raised Sabarat up, pointed to the back of his head and exclaimed: "Look here!"

There was a severe and bloody bruise, which had been made by a violent blow with a hammer or a club, at the base of the man's skull.

Gautrais, who had picked up the revolver, opened the cylinder – all six cartridges were intact. Showing the revolver to his companions, he said: "He must have been surprised, he has not even had time to defend himself." Scarcely had he said these words than Sabarat half opened his eyes; his hand, which seemed to have gained a little strength, caught hold of the arm of the man who supported him. His lips moved; a deep, hoarse sigh escaped him and, in a very faint voice, with the death-rattle gathering in his throat, he cried: "The ghost! the ghost!" Then his limbs went into terrible contortions; his head slumped forwards; a pinkish froth erupted from his half-opened mouth.

The head guard, Sabarat, was dead!

CHAPTER II
JACQUES BELLEGARDE

The same evening, about seven o'clock, at the police headquarters, M. Ferval, the Superintendent, conducted an important interview in his office with M. Lavergne and his assistant. It is needless to add that the subject under discussion was the drama which took place in the Louvre the preceding night.

While waiting outside the room for official news, representatives of the Parisian and provincial press gave varied and contradictory reports of the incident. Noisy discussions took place. In fact, they became so noisy that the office boy was sent to ask them to be a little more quiet. Seated somewhat apart from the rest was a young man of about thirty years of age. He had a very intelligent face, and seemed to pay no attention to the babel around him.

The man was Jacques Bellegarde, the brilliant editor of *Le Petit Parisien*. He was a man of few words, decisive action, and profound thoughts. Having a liking for all mysteries, the unfolding enigma of the Louvre phantom, although he knew no more of it than his colleagues, awakened a great interest in him.

A big, broad-shouldered fellow, whom his companions had nicknamed "Amer Menthe", approached Bellegarde and, knocking him cordially on the shoulder, said: "So, what do you think about this story?"

"Nothing yet."

"Come now."

"And you?"

"It bores me," declared Amer Menthe.

Bellegarde was just going to reply when a door opened and M. Lavergne and his assistant came out.

All the reporters immediately surrounded the officials and hurled questions at them.

"Gentlemen! I beg you," pleaded M. Lavergne, trying to disengage himself.

M. Lavergne referred the reporters to an inspector who had just come out of the interview room – a man with piercing eyes, a tall figure, and a moustache like a American: "Here is M. Menardier, one of our best inspectors, who is going to look into this affair; without doubt, he can give you information better than we can."

The reporters immediately left M. Lavergne and surrounded Menardier, but in a firm tone Menardier declared that he had nothing more to tell them.

Menardier turned to the governor and his assistant and said: "I should be glad if you would adopt the same attitude."

Bellegarde said: "You are not very kind to the press, M. Menardier."

The inspector replied brusquely: "In this business, more than any other, one has to use discretion. It is no affair of yours – it is purely my own concern."

Whereupon Bellegarde said with a smile: "And I am going to know of it also."

Menardier left them and overtook M. Lavergne and his assistant. Bellegarde rushed after him and caught up just as he was again impressing M. Lavergne of the importance in not divulging anything regarding the affair. Menardier frowned when he saw the journalist. "Rest assured, my dear sir," said Bellegarde, "I have no intention of following you."

He went away after having politely raised his hat.

"I wish that man were out of the way," grumbled Menardier. "I feel he wants to catch me out."

Bellegarde, after trying in vain to get into the Louvre, decided to walk back to his office at *Le Petit Parisien*. As he walked along, he heard newspaper boys calling out the third edition of an evening paper. Everybody was buying a paper – evidently to read the latest news regarding the murder at the museum.

Very shortly he reached his office. After having read his correspondence, he sat down at his desk and thought for a few moments, and then composed an article which read as follows:

"Is it a question of a lone criminal; or is it a new exploit of the international gang who have been robbing museums in Italy? In any case, we are able to affirm that there is no ghost at the Louvre, only a thief and assassin."

As he was putting his signature at the end, somebody knocked at the door – it was an office boy, who brought in an envelope which Bellegarde hurriedly opened. To his surprise, he found in it a piece of blue paper on which was written:

"I warn you that if you continue to interest yourself the affair of the Louvre, I will not hesitate to send you to join the guard, Sabarat.
BELPHEGOR."

"Belphegor!" said Jacques with surprise; "Ah! what does that signify?"

Scarcely had he uttered these words than his telephone rang. Bellegarde lifted the receiver and heard the shrill and impatient voice of a woman.

"Is it you, Jacques? Hallo, it is I, Simone."

"Are you well, *ma petite*?" replied the reporter without enthusiasm.

"I wanted to remind you that I am having some friends tonight. I can rely on you coming, can't I?"

Visibly irritated, Bellegarde replied: "I am very busy with the Louvre incident."

"What incident?"

"Ah! you do not know. Well, read *Le Petit Parisien* tomorrow."

"However, you will come?" she pleaded.

"If I am able to, I promise you," replied the reporter.

"You'll be able to come if you wish to."

"I shall be rather late."

"That's all right, provided you come. See you soon, *cheri*."

"*Au revoir*."

Bellegarde hung up the telephone. A great weariness came over him. He shook himself as if he wished to throw off some weight from his shoulders. With a nervous gesture, he re-read the strange message which he had just received, repeating the words aloud:

"I will not hesitate to send you to join the guard, Sabarat. Belphegor."

Then, with a determined look in his eyes, the young journalist exclaimed: "Well, Lord Belphegor, I accept your challenge – and we will see which of us is the stronger."

CHAPTER III
SIMONE DESROCHES

That same evening, about eleven o'clock, a reception was being given in a luxurious house situated in the Rue Boileau, Auteuil. The reception was given by the owner of the house, Simone Desroches, a young poetess. She was holding it to celebrate the completion of her latest piece of poetry.

Simone was a girl of remarkable beauty; in her dress of white she looked very like a Shakespearean faery.

Shortly after eleven, she began to recite her verse, in a monotonous voice:

"My soul is a fortress
Which I have made the garden of my heart;
My heart is the terrestrial garden
Where strange flowers wither..."

Obviously, Simone had no talent as a poetess – although she thought she was a very clever one! Her many admirers were attracted either by her beauty or her huge fortune – certainly not by her poems.

Simone was the child of a well-known Paris banker. She had lost her mother very early in life. Her father, entirely absorbed by his business, had entrusted her education and care to an instructress of Scandinavian nationality – Madam Elsa Bergen.

Simone's father died very soon after she was twenty-one years of age. She then decided to live her own way – she was very independent and had a romantic nature. Possessing a huge fortune, she had bought this plush abode in Auteuil, where she resided with Elsa Bergen.

At this reception, amongst her many admirers, one noticed a certain Maurice de Thouars; he came from a very old family who were in poor circumstances. He also represented a firm of motor-car dealers, who badly needed capital. He was very handsome – in fact, a ladies' man of some repute – and consequently a very vain person; he once thought that he had only to say the word to the beautiful Simone and she would fall into his arms. However, to his great dismay, Simone had told him that she neither neither husband nor lover. She said she wanted to have complete freedom.

Nevertheless, three months after that, Simone Desroches fell violently in love with Jacques Bellegarde.

They met in Syria, where Simone was travelling and where Bellegarde was on business for *Le Petit Parisien*. They were friends at first, but very soon their friendship ripened into love. However, since their return to Paris, Simone had shown herself in quite a different light – she was jealous and tyrannical, and she killed all the love that Bellegarde had for her. Simone became more and more attached to Bellegarde and hoped to marry him, but Bellegarde refused to marry her in spite of her riches, and in spite of having only his gift for writing as his fortune. Then there were some fearful scenes, and Bellegarde thought of breaking off the relationship. Only one thing stopped him – he was afraid lest Simone should commit suicide, as she had often threatened to do.

When he arrived at the reception, Simone had just finished reciting her poetry amidst loud applause from her guests.

As soon as she saw Jacques she blushed to the roots of her hair, but everyone attributed this to the applause which she received for her recitation. The applause did not affect her; she had eyes only for Jacques, and his company was all she desired.

The guests had gathered round her and imprisoned her. Some aesthetes wanted to kiss her hands. Baron Papillon, the rich collector, and the Baroness, as snobbish as they were rich and foolish, congratulated her and tried to impress on her that they were great critics of art. The handsome Maurice de Thouars, who had succeeded in getting near the poetess, offered her the warmest compliments, but Simone avoided him, saying: "I beg you to leave me alone."

She quickly joined Jacques Bellegarde and offered him her hand, saying in a low voice: "Ah, here you are! At last!"

Then looking at him with a tender reproach in her eyes, she added in a still low voice: "Why are you so late?

"I have not been able–"

'You are going to stay?"

"It is impossible... this affair at the Louvre."

"A pretext."

"I assure you that it is very serious, Let me tell you about it."

"Please don't bother."

"Why?"

"Because I want to spare you a lie."

"You will see tomorrow in the newspapers–"

"I never read the newspapers."

The poetess and the reporter continued to talk in a low tone. Maurice de Thouars, who observed them with a jealous expression on his face, went towards a woman of about fifty years of age, whose hair was nearly white and who had a very hard face. She had held herself very aloof since the commencement of the evening. It was Elsa Bergen, Simone's companion.

The aesthetes at the reception continued to eat and drink heartily. One young man, with a handsome profile and immaculately dressed, was artfully and cleverly pocketing a set of silver spoons. A virtuoso, in a grave and bored air, sat down at a grand piano to play. Everyone turned to look at him, expecting to hear some good music, but they were disappointed – the pianist gave a most awful performance.

Baron Papillon, deafened by the dreadful noise, approached Simone and said:

"Who is this virtuoso?"

Simone replied, "A young Czecho-Slovakian named Dmitrà Morovanov."

"I do not know him."

"I am just bringing him out."

"You believe him talented?"

"He is a genius."

Noticing that Simone was absorbed in the playing of Morovanov, Jacques Bellegarde took the opportunity of making his departure. Just as he went out of the door, Simone looked up and saw him disappear. A faint cry escaped her and her eyes filled with tears. She sat down and hid her face in her hands.

"What an artiste!" murmured Baron Papillon to his wife.

"Simone looks as though she is crying," said the Baroness.

Simone was indeed crying, but she was not crying over

Morovanov's music; she was crying over her unrequited love – her broken dream!

Jacques Bellegarde soon arrived home. After a good night's rest, he got up ready to continue his investigation into the Louvre ghost incident.

As he passed out of his dressing-room into his dining-room, he saw his housekeeper sitting in an armchair and reading *Le Petit Parisien*. She was also the wife of Pierre Gautrais, the keeper of the Louvre.

Absorbed in her paper, Marie-Jeanne did not see him come in. He regarded her amusedly, then suddenly he clapped his hands. She jumped up in great fear and exclaimed:

"The ghost!"

On recognizing the reporter, she put her hand on her heart as if to steady its beatings.

"Excuse me, Mr. Jacques, I was just reading your article." Putting the paper on the table, she was just going out of the room when Jacques called her back.

"One moment, Madame Gautrais."

"At your service, Mr. Jacques," said the good woman.

Bellegarde thought for a few seconds, then said: "Can you render me a service?"

"With pleasure, Mr. Jacques; you are so kind to me. Thanks to you, I am able to go to the theatre for nothing. Believe me, it is my duty–"

With a friendly gesture, the reporter stopped her never-ending speech and in a grave voice said:

"It is necessary that your husband helps me to hide tonight in the Room of the Barbarous Gods."

"Heavens!" cried Marie-Jeanne, "that would not be right."

Jacques insisted.

"But if–"

"I want to try, only–"

A bell rang.

"Go and see who it is," said the journalist; "but I am not seeing anyone."

The housekeeper returned almost immediately, saying in a

hostile tone:

"It is *she* again!"

Jacques made an irritated gesture. As he nervously extinguished his lighted cigarette the housekeeper said: "Shall I tell her you are not here?"

"No," replied Jacques. "She would be capable of waiting for me outside. Ask her into my office."

When Marie-Jeanne had gone, the reporter muttered between his teeth: "This woman leads me an awful life. This must be finished."

After pacing his room and trying to work out how he could break with Simone without causing too much disturbance, he opened the door of his office. Miss Desroches, who appeared very upset, came towards him, and briskly drawing a note from her bag, handed it to him, saying in a trembling voice:

"This is what I have just received."

Jacques took the note and read as follows:

"MADEMOISELLE
I know that you are very much interested in Mr. Jacques Bellegarde...
and I advise you to use all your influence in preventing him from
meddling in the affair of the Louvre – otherwise he is a dead man!
BELPHEGOR."

"I beg you to give up this business," said Simone.

"You are ridiculous; it is not possible," replied Jacques.

"You do not love me any more," said the young woman. She then fell on to a chair and burst into tears.

Bellegarde, annoyed, went up to her. Then he said: "Come, come! Let us be reasonable!"

She replied: "I adore you."

Jacques slowly managed to take his hands out of his mistress's grasp; he went to his desk, opened a drawer, put inside it the note which Simone had given him, and then locked it.

Simone, whose eyes had not left him, murmured:

"I feel that all is finished."

She got up and Bellegarde weakly attempted to stop her.

"Good-bye," said she in an unsteady voice. There was such

distress in her voice that Jacques prevented her going. She collapsed in his arms.

He could not help but feel sorry for her, and when she recovered he offered to take her to lunch. Simone accepted with joy, and they decided to go to the Restaurant Glycines.

A sudden joy flooded Simone's the face. Jacques gave her a kiss on her feverish forehead, and then he rang for Marie-Jeanne.

"My stick; my hat," he said.

Simone took her powder-box out of her handbag and tried to remove the traces of weeping.

When the housekeeper returned with Jacques's things, he whispered into her ear:

"Be sure not to forget to ask your husband."

Madame Gautrais made a gesture of acquiescence; then Jacques and Simone went out.

As Madame Gautrais watched them go, she muttered to herself:

"He must have much courage – to pass the day with a woman such as she, and then to pass the night in the Room of the Barbarous Gods!"

CHAPTER IV
THE RESTAURANT GLYCINES

The Restaurant Glycines was the most fashionable in the Bois de Boulogne. It was a wonderful spring day, and the restaurant was filled with denizens of the fashionable world, most of whom, taking advantage of the gorgeous weather, sat and lunched in the magnificent garden.

An immaculately dressed, elderly man, who had a grey beard and wore spectacles, entered Glycines accompanied by a charming young girl who carried a parasol. She really was very pretty, and was dressed exquisitely. Their entrance was unnoticed, even by Bellegarde and Simone, who were lunching at the next table. The proprietor offered a menu to the young girl, but she passed it on to the old gentleman and said in a clear, musical voice:

"You order, papa; you know this restaurant better than I do."

"Very well, Colette."

At these words, Jacques slowly turned his head. He could not help showing some surprise... he had just recognized the charming young lady from the day before, whom he had met in the Boulevard Sebastopol.

When she saw him, she gave him a quick smile and then, lowering her eyes while her father ordered from the menu, she took one of the pinks from her table and raised it to her face, seeming to take great pleasure in smelling it. Simone, always very much awake, had perceived this little incident.

"Do you know these people?" said Simone to Jacques.

"Not at all!" replied Jacques, in an indifferent voice.

From time to time, Jacques could not help looking furtively in the direction of the young girl. Suddenly, Simone looked at him, and said: "Do you still intend to investigate this Louvre affair?"

The old gentleman and his daughter evidently heard this, for they exchanged a rapid glance.

Jacques did not reply to Simone's question. Simone became more and more agitated, and said:

"You might at least listen when I speak."

Jacques started, then he said in an annoyed tone:

"What did you say?"

"Nothing," replied Simone in a sullen voice.

The proprietor of the premises, with a grand air, served up the quenelles. Bellegarde turned his head slowly towards the next table. Colette continued to speak to her father in a confidential manner. In a little while she raised her eyes and looked coquettishly at the journalist who, in spite of himself, could not help smiling at her. This was too much for Simone. Angrily throwing her serviette on the table, she said: "I have had enough of this."

"Come, come! what is the matter now?" said Jacques disconcertedly.

In an aggressive voice, Simone replied: "Because a young girl with no manners makes eyes at you, you imagine yourself at once—"

"Simone, what do you mean?"

"Excuse me – I saw you."

Jacques tried to calm her, but in vain. She got up and, gathering up her handbag and trembling the while with anger, she said in a very rude voice: "This finishes it. Good-bye."

She stormed out after throwing Colette a thunderous look; and Bellegarde, taken aback, had done nothing to prevent her from going.

Just as he was going to apologize for this incident to his neighbours, who pretended not to notice the insult, a commissionaire called out.

"M. Claude Barjac is wanted on the telephone."

The old gentleman got up immediately and followed the commissionaire. Colette stayed alone and glanced at the journalist, who continued to eat his quenelles in a preoccupied manner. He looked very annoyed.

A minute or two later, Jacques looked up and again met the young girl's encouraging smile: he was just going to speak to her, but M. Barjac had returned and, seating himself in front of his daughter, murmured to her: "It is for tonight."

With a quick glance, Colette pointed out the reporter to her father, and M. Barjac cunningly smiled.

Jacques then took some paper from his pocket-book and, with

the aid of his pen, wrote the following letter:

"MY DEAR SIMONE
Although it gives me much pain to make you unhappy, I simply cannot put up with your continued fits of jealousy, which are quite unjustifiable."

The proprietor interrupted Jacques, and passed him the menu again.

"And now, what will Monsieur choose?" he asked.

"I have finished," replied Bellegarde. "Give me the bill."

Then he continued to write:

"It will therefore be better that we see no more of each other, as we do not understand one another. Goodbye,
 JACQUES."

The reporter sealed up his letter and traced the address with his pen. A waiter brought him his bill, which he quickly settled. After he had been to the cloak-room to get his coat and hat, he went up to the restaurant proprietor and asked him if he knew who the old gentleman and young girl were who had dined at the next table to him.

The proprietor replied:

"I do not know, sir. It is the first time they have been to this restaurant."

Before Jacques went out of the restaurant, he gave one more glance in the direction of Colette, who prettily smiled at him and blushed.

When he had gone, Colette sighed and murmured to herself: "Poor boy, it is a pity."

She turned to her father, who was making some notes in his pocket-book, and said to him: "You say that it is for tonight?"

Barjac replied in a grave tone:

"I will tell you all about it later;" and he added in a mysterious tone, "here, the walls may have ears."

CHAPTER V

Marie-Jeanne felt very anxious. It was one o'clock in the afternoon, and her husband had not yet returned.

Her presentiments had never ceased to torment her since the supposed visit of the ghost, and still more since the assassination of the unfortunate Sabarat.

There was a sudden knock at the door.

"My God!" thought Marie-Jeanne, "supposing someone should bring him back to me on a stretcher!"

She quickly opened the door. It was her neighbour, Madame Roublet, a little old woman who had the most malicious tongue within miles around.

"Ah! it is you," said Marie-Jeanne, in a voice with no welcome in it.

The woman held a newspaper in her hand, and with a wicked smile asked in a sweet but hypocritical voice:

"Has your husband returned yet?"

"No."

"Wait! wait!" said Madame Roublet. "Haven't you seen the newspaper?" And without even waiting for Madame Gautrais to reply, she showed her the end of an article which read:

"The Inspector Menardier seems more and more convinced that the thief who broke into the Louvre has accomplices in the place."

''Well!" said Marie-Jeanne, returning the newspaper to the woman, who was obviously hinting that she thought her husband would be suspected. She retorted indignantly: "He – the most honest man in the world."

Madame Roublet replied: "Things like that do sometimes happen!"

"You're just a malicious old woman," said the guard's wife; and seizing her neighbour by the arm. she pushed her towards the door.

A few seconds after, a loud voice was heard, and Pierre Gautrais appeared. On seeing him, Madam Gautrais dropped Madame

Roublet on the ground, and the latter said to her husband: "You've got a harpy – not a wife."

Madame Gautrais, still trembling, said: "She came tell me that it was you who was the phantom of the Louvre!"

"It is not true," replied the neighbour, "she is a liar."

"Liar yourself, you old hag!" said Marie-Jeanne.

Gautrais opened the door wide and ordered the old busybody to get out – and it didn't take her long to do it!

Then Madame Gautrais said to her husband: "Any news?"

"There is. This morning, Inspector Menardier, a sneaky old man, questioned me in the presence of the chief curator. I told him all I knew."

"And then?"

"He made notes in his notebook, looking at me sideways all the while. Oh! his look! He seemed to look right through me... then he asked me suddenly: 'Weren't you on bad terms with the head guard, Sabarat?' I replied that, on the contrary, we were on very good terms, and that I had even offered to spend the night with him in the Room of the Barbarous Gods, but that Sabarat had not wished me to do so."

"What did he reply to that?"

"Nothing."

"I don't see that that need worry you, my poor husband."

"It was the way in which he looked at me."

"Then you really think that he suspected you," exclaimed Marie-Jeanne, "I should like to see anyone accuse you, indeed!" She tossed her head in the air and said: "Luckily, we have some friends in the press."

"M. Bellegarde," said Gautrais.

"Exactly," replied Marie-Jeanne. And leaning towards her husband, she said to him in a confidential tone: "He has asked me if you would kindly help him to get into the Room of the Barbarous Gods tonight."

"Why?"

"Probably because he wants to solve the mystery of the phantom."

Gautrais replied firmly: "I can do nothing."

When his wife insisted, he said: "I don't want to lose my job because of Bellegarde."

"But he is a very nice young man."

"He may be!"

"He might be useful to us."

"I doubt it."

And bringing his fist down upon the table, he said vexedly: "Now, that is enough! We'll have nothing to do with it."

* * * * *

The Louvre Museum was re-opened to the public the next morning, with the exception of the Room of the Barbarous Gods, the door of which had been hermetically sealed. The public arrived early in the vain hope of learning or seeing something of the phantom. The mystery was really unfathomable.

Inspector Menardier had not been idle. Not having discovered, after a minute examination, any traces of burglary in the old museum, the detective came to the logical conclusion that Sabarat's killer must have had an accomplice in the place. First of all he suspected Gautrais, even though he knew of his good conduct in the past. However, when he made inquiries concerning him, he found that he had not left his home during that night. So it was no use suspecting him!

Menardier realized that he had a very artful and clever adversary to catch. However, the first thing for him to do was to find out how he had entered the Louvre and got out again so easily – and so he decided to be there on the next night, with several chosen detectives. With this object in view, he begged M. Lavergne to give him the plans of the museum, which he studied with great care.

Mr. Jacques Bellegarde was also determined, as much as ever, to elucidate this mystery, and he had not been idle, either.

After going to the offices of *Le Petit Parisien* in order to read through his post, he arrived at the Louvre. It was three o'clock when he got there. He went immediately to the Room of the Barbarous Gods, but found that it was impossible to enter. Two armed detectives stood by the entrance door, and there was an improvised wooden barrier placed round it.

The young reporter then rushed off to find Gautrais, feeling confident that the request which he had asked Marie-Jeanne to make of him would be granted. Passing through the antiques gallery, he was advancing quickly towards the statue of Venus de Milo, when he suddenly stopped, dumb-founded.

Seated on a camp-stool, with a sketch-book on her knee and a pencil in her hand, was the charming Parisienne whom he had made the acquaintance of the day before in the Boulevard Sebastopol and who, two hours previously, had provoked Simone at the Restaurant Glycines, She was drinking in the beauty of the divine statue.

Jacques hesitated a moment, then going up to her and saluting her in a lordly manner, he said: "Really, Mademoiselle, we seem destined to meet."

"Indeed, Monsieur," replied Colette with a gracious smile, and she added: "I have seen your portrait on the cover of one of your books. I might say that I read all your articles, and must confess that they interest me very much."

"You are very flattering, Mademoiselle," said the reporter. "By the way, I want to apologize to you regarding the unfortunate incident at the restaurant today." He stopped, feeling a little embarrassed.

Colette then said, still smiling and pretending to be surprised: "Monsieur, I don't know what you mean."

Jacques thought it better not to allude again to the incident, and said, glancing at the sketch book which Colette held on her knee:

"You are very talented, Mademoiselle."

The young girl burst our laughing, and giving the journalist a page from her sketch book, which showed only a few pencil strokes, she said. "You see... I have not yet commenced."

A little flustered by his blunder, Bellegarde said the first thing that came into his head: "Then, Mademoiselle, you have no fear of ghosts."

Colette replied gaily: "I can hardly believe there are such things."

"However, it appears that there is one at the Louvre."

"Yes; so I understand."

"I have resolved to try and find it."

"Well, I hope you do, Monsieur Bellegarde."

And, taking up her pencil, the pretty Parisienne commenced to sketch, thereby giving Bellegarde a hint that the conversation – so far as she was concerned – was ended.

Jacques was too gentlemanly to trespass further on her time and, after having saluted her, he went away, but not without a tinge of regret.

When he had disappeared, a man who had concealed himself behind a statue and had observed the two young people talking, came out of his hiding-place.

It was Claude Barjac.

As her father approached her, Colette blushed deeply. He asked her in a grave tone what Bellegarde had said. She was just going to reply when Gautrais suddenly appeared from a neighbouring room, looking very scared. He raised his hat and said to Barjac:

"Sir, may I have a word with you?"

With a brief gesture, Colette's father invited him to speak.

"This journalist who spoke to Mademoiselle just now–"

"Yes, well?"

"He has asked me if I would get him into the Room of the Barbarous Gods tonight."

"Well!"

"He is waiting for my reply."

"Well!" said Barjac in an imperative tone, "go and tell him that you will do so."

"But, sir..." stammered the guard, taken by surprise.

"Do what I tell you and don't argue," said Barjac. Gautrais hurriedly departed.

Then Colette got up and said to her father: "I wish no harm to come to Monsieur Bellegarde."

"Are you interested in him, then?" asked Barjac, raising his eyebrows.

Outwardly off-hand, the young girl replied: "I have read his articles; his books; and I think he is very clever; also I must confess that he is very kind towards me."

CHAPTER VI

That same evening, about eleven o'clock, a man stealthily crossed the great courtyard of the Louvre. He was dressed in a dark overcoat, the collar of which was turned up, and he wore a dark felt hat which was placed well down over his ears.

He went up to a figure who was hiding behind a pilaster. This person, without saying a word, made a sign to the man in the dark overcoat to follow him. Then, with a bundle of keys, he carefully opened a door and went with his companion into the vestibule, which was in front of the Galerie des Antiques.

Both men crept noiselessly into the gallery. After removing the wooden barrier from the entrance door of the Room of the Barbarous Gods, they unlocked it and entered. It was almost totally dark.

The man with the bunch of keys appeared to be very edgy, and looked around him nervously. Then he murmured:

"Monsieur Bellegarde, my services are required elsewhere, otherwise I should have been pleased to stay with you."

"It is unnecessary, my dear Gautrais," replied the journalist, and, drawing a pistol from his coat pocket, he added: "I am on my guard. Ghost or thief, I don't think he will have the impudence to return to the Louvre tonight. Anyhow, should he turn up, I am here to receive him."

He shook the keeper by the hand and said:

"Believe me, I will not forget the service which you have rendered me. Thanks to you, I feel that I am going to make some precious discoveries which will perhaps be more than a match for our friend, Monsieur Menardier."

Gautrais nodded his head dubiously; then he went away, leaving the intrepid reporter all alone.

A moonbeam shone through one of the large, high windows.

"A ray of light," said Bellegarde. "Is it a symbol?"

He looked around, vaguely distinguishing the silhouettes of the Gods, which looked very mysterious and weird in the dim light.

The moonlight fell upon the statue of the demon Belphegor, and Bellegarde examined it very carefully. He murmured: "What a

27

great pity it is, my old Belphegor; you write so well and yet you cannot speak! You must know everything about the affair which we are investigating."

Bellegarde suddenly remembered the ancient history of this medieval statue, which came from the Cathedral of Dol, in Brittany. Centuries ago, purely by chance, a sacristan had discovered inside the statue a secret chamber which contained several hundred pieces of gold. Bellegarde murmured: "Have you, by any chance, a secret place inside you now which contains anything of interest to us? After all, there would be nothing extraordinary in that. Let us then look, to see what this divinity may be hiding in its stomach or its head."

And taking from his overcoat pocket a little electric torch, he flashed it slowly all over the statue.

He peered into the demonic face, which was clenched in a most terrible rictus. The centuries which had elapsed had scarcely rendered its features more beautiful.

Bellegarde was examining the statue very carefully when suddenly, behind him, a shape appeared, robed in a dark shroud and wearing a hood which looked like a mask, through which one could just perceive two shining eyes. It was the Phantom of the Louvre, just as Pierre Gautrais had described to his superiors.

Holding a club in its right, black-gloved hand, silently – as if its feet did not touch the ground – it advanced towards Jacques who, absorbed in his examination, could neither see nor hear it.

Just as the night-prowler reached Bellegarde, and was going to give him a terrific blow with his club, a man darted out from behind a mass of stone and, seizing it by the wrist, cried in a loud voice: "Thief; I've got you!"

Jacques stood up with a start and gave an awful shout. By the light of the moon he could just perceive, two steps away from him, a pair of figures – one was Claude Barjac, father of Colette, and the other – the Phantom of the Louvre!

With a cat-like movement, the Phantom escaped from Barjac's grasp and, like a flash of lightning, raced towards the staircase of the Victoire de Samothrace.

Jacques, who had instinctively seized his pistol, fired it in the direction of the Phantom, who had already disappeared into the darkness.

Barjac and Bellegarde hurried in pursuit. Bellegarde saw him mounting the stairs four at a time, and quickly followed him, but just as he reached him, the Phantom turned upon him, and gave him a most terrific blow with the club, which threw him to the ground in a dazed condition. Fortunately, the blow had not badly injured him.

Some lights then appeared at the top of the staircase. It was Menardier and his men who, while they were exploring the gallery of Apollon, had heard the commotion and at once ran to the rescue with lanterns.

The Phantom was just disappearing when Claude Barjac ran up the stairs and cried: "Bar the way; hold him!"

But, with a great bound, the Phantom threw himself out of the lantern-light and disappeared into a great void of shadows to the left of them.

Bellegarde by now had come to, and got up from the ground. He was trying to work out how the Phantom had come to escape him, when Inspector Menardier and his men approached him, and Menardier said in an angry voice: "Monsieur Bellegarde, you here! You are a suspected person, and I must arrest you."

"One moment," intervened Barjac, who had rejoined the group.

"I beg you not to arrest this man. I was hidden in the Room of the Barbarous Gods, and I can assure you that, without my help, this unfortunate man would have suffered just as the keeper, Sabarat, has done."

At the sight of this new personage, whom he did not know, Menardier said in a threatening voice: "First of all, who are you?"

With a brusque gesture, Barjac pulled off his artificial beard and jokingly replied: "My dear Menardier, I think we have failed in our game."

"Chantecoq!" exclaimed the surprised Menardier, while Bellegarde, no less surprised, said: "Chantecoq! The great Chantecoq! King of detectives!"

CHAPTER VII

Chantecoq, who had just played this unexpected rôle in the drama of the Louvre, was none other than the old detective of the "Sûreté Générale" who, before the War, was a real celebrity owing to his many famous exploits.

Chantecoq was mobilized in 1914 as a Reserve officer. He won the Legion d'Honneur and the Croix de Guerre. He established himself as a private detective after the Armistice and took as his secretary, or more precisely as his collaborator, his daughter, Colette, who was very eager to assist him.

Chantecoq was not only well-known as a detective; people knew him as a man of courage and loyalty, to whom they entrusted their greatest secrets.

How did Chantecoq come to be mixed up in this affair? In a few words:

Chantecoq had been ordered by the Italian Government to find a thief, who, after committing a daring larceny in a Florence museum, had hidden himself in Paris. Perhaps this thief was also the Phantom of the Louvre. The great detective immediately came to see the keeper, Pierre Gautrais, who had served under his orders during the war, and whose life he had saved.

Gautrais thought very highly of his old chief, and he was very keen to hear his views, since that he felt that Inspector Menardier vaguely suspected him; Gautrais thought that Chantecoq could not fail to elucidate the ghostly mystery.

The next day the great detective was working in his office, which was situated on the ground floor of a little house in the Avenue de Verzy. He also resided at the house.

His office was a large room which was tastefully furnished, and the walls were lined with beautifully bound books.

He was sitting in front of his desk, and was just summing up the events of the preceding day, when a door suddenly opened and Colette entered and looked at her father with an expression of great tenderness.

Chantecoq, deep in thought, had not noticed her presence. Colette crept softly up to him and threw her arms round his neck. The detective immediately took a revolver out of his pocket and, turning round, threatened her with it.

Colette, feigning great terror, hurriedly held up her hands. Then the detective calmly opened his revolver and took from it – a cigarette!

Colette burst out laughing, and said: "I have not seen this novelty before."

"A present from the Countess de Morange," replied Chantecoq.

"Ah, yes! The great lady whose pearl necklace you restored to her. Very amusing; very original!"

"Isn't it? Now, stop laughing, little girl; we have work to do."

"I think," said Colette, "that we have found a rather difficult adversary."

Chantecoq was silent.

"And you, papa, what do you think?" questioned the young girl.

"I don't know what to think yet," replied the detective, who wore an expression on his face which reflected the doubt and anxiety which were on his mind.

He got up brusquely and commenced to pace slowly up and down his office. Then, after a moment or two, he said: "Why did this villain target a cumbersome statue which would be so difficult to remove? Why didn't he choose a picture or some precious object instead; and how did he enter, and how did he get out of the place?"

As Chantecoq spoke he approached his daughter who was sitting at the desk, leaning her elbows on it in deep thought. Chantecoq put his hand on her shoulder and said: "Well, little one, what do you think?"

Colette awoke from her reverie and replied: "I don't know what to think about it.".

Chantecoq affectionately patted her cheek and said: "I rather believe that you were thinking of the handsome young man."

"Father!" protested the young girl, blushing.

"Never mind," said the detective with a whimsical smile, "it will not be long before you see him again."

And, picking up a letter which lay on his desk he handed it to his daughter, saying: "Read this message, which I have just received."

It was worded as follows:

"31, Avenue d'Antin,
Tel. Elysee 86.29
DEAR M. CHANTECOQ – Something unforeseen has happened to prevent me from keeping my appointment of this morning which we arranged at the Louvre last night. Would you therefore kindly see me this afternoon at three o'clock instead?
Yours sincerely,
JACQUES BELLEGARDE
P.S. I tried to get you over the telephone, but could get no answer, so I am sending you this note which I hope will reach you in good time."

"Really!" said Chantecoq, "the telephone service gets worse and worse. I am going to complain about it."

"Please don't father," said Colette, "it was my fault – I took the receiver off its hook."

"Why?"

"You returned so late, and slept so well this morning that I didn't want anyone to disturb you."

"Oh, indeed!" said the detective, with a smile. "Well, now, please telephone Monsieur Bellegarde and tell him that it will be convenient to see him this afternoon at three o'clock."

Colette took up the receiver and dialled Bellegarde's number.

"Hello! hello!"

"Monsieur Bellegarde?" asked Colette.

"Speaking, Mademoiselle."

"This is Monsieur Chantecoq's secretary speaking; he wishes me to tell you that it will be convenient for him to see you here at three o'clock this afternoon."

"That's good! I will come. And, Mademoiselle, wilt you please apologize to Monsieur Chantecoq for my not having kept the appointment arranged for this morning?"

"I will, Monsieur."

"Thank you very much, Mademoiselle."

Colette put up the receiver. Chantecoq, raising his head, said to her: "Well, my little one, are you happy?"

Colette knocked some papers which lay on the desk on to the ground. As she picked them up, her father noticed the excited state she was in. When she had put them in order, she reminded her father of the fact that they had work to do.

CHAPTER VIII
THE MYSTERIOUS HUNCHBACK

Just about this time, outside Bellegarde's house, an odd-looking personage was loitering, dressed in dark clothes. He was a hunchback, and had very hard, sharp features. His feet and hands were enormous, and his legs were heavily bowed. It appeared as if he was trying to repair the rear tyre of a small motor-car. Every now and then he would glance towards Bellegarde's window, where he could see, through the transparent curtains, the figures of a man and woman who appeared to be animatedly discussing something – they were none other than Jacques Bellegarde and Simone Desroches's companion, Elsa Bergen.

The night before, the reporter had found a note from Elsa Bergen intimating that she would be calling on him in the morning to see him about something very important. Suspecting that something very serious had happened, Jacques thought the best thing to do was to cancel his appointment with Monsieur Chantecoq, and to ask him to be good enough to see him in the afternoon.

Elsa Bergen was not in her usual calm state.

"Monsieur," she had said, "if you had been there, you would certainly have taken pity on poor Simone. During the whole day she did not stop crying. She passed a dreadful night. Fortunately, I managed to get her revolver away from her, and also a phial of laudanum which she had hidden in the bottom of her wardrobe. Monsieur jacques, it is absolutely necessary that you come to see her again."

"Mademoiselle," said the reporter, "what you tell me grieves me very much; but remember, if Simone is unhappy, it is more her fault than mine." And with an expression of absolute sincerity, Bellegarde continued: "You, and everyone, know how tyrannical and absolutely impossible she has been of late. Yesterday, at the Restaurant Glycines, where I took her to lunch, she made a scene which placed me in a very awkward position."

"I do not deny that Simone is very difficult; I leave it to your conscience to tell you whether you should come and see her or not."

Jacques thought over Elsa Bergen's last words.

He could not bear to have on his conscience the death of this girl – yet, at the same time, he did not wish to resume relations with her when he no longer loved her. But had he the right to inflict such suffering upon her, which would perhaps result in her committing suicide?

At this terrible thought he could not help saying; "As she is so ill, Mademoiselle, I will call round see her very shortly."

"You will save her," replied Elsa Bergen, offering her hand. "I will go at once and tell her the good news."

Bellegarde accompanied her to the door, then he returned to his study.

He thought of the charming girl whom he had he chanced to meet three times just lately. What a contrast to Simone! He imagined that to have the love of a girl such as Colette must be sublime. But still, perhaps she was in love with – and loved by – someone already!

There was a knock on the door.

"Come in," said Bellegarde.

It was Marie-Jeanne. Her plump face had lost its usual gay and open expression, and her eyes looked as if she had been crying.

"Monsieur Jacques," declared she, "excuse me if I'm late, but something has happened at home."

"Whatever is the matter?" replied Bellegarde in a disturbed voice.

"My husband was called away early this morning see the Curator of the Louvre... he was asked if he let you and Monsieur Chantecoq into the Room the Barbarous Gods."

"Well?" questioned Bellegarde.

"He owned up that he did so, and now he's been dismissed," said Marie-Jeanne, trying to hide her tears.

"My good Marie-Jeanne," said Jacques, "I am so very sorry. But don't upset yourself; I will recommend Gautrais to the board of *Le Petit Parisien*, and I'm sure that they will find him a position just as good as the one which he has lost."

"Monsieur Jacques, I knew that I could count on you," replied the woman, giving Bellegarde a grateful look.

He went towards the door and, turning round, said: "Good-bye, Marie-Jeanne. Tell your husband to come and see me to-night about eight o'clock at *Le Petit Parisien* offices."

"I will tell him, Monsieur Jacques; and thank you."

Bellegarde took his hat, overcoat, and portmanteau, and went out.

The mysterious hunchback had at last finished repairing his tyre; he was now examining the engine of his car. On seeing the journalist, he quickly closed up the bonnet of the vehicle and got into the driver's seat.

Jacques hailed a passing taxi and gave the driver Simone's address. The hunchback put his own car into action and followed the taxi.

Meanwhile, Marie-Jeanne, who needed some air, had opened the window, and as she did so she saw the hunchback disappearing.

"A hunchback," she thought. "What a pity I could not touch his hump. People say that freaks bring good luck." Then she added: "But I feel that this affair will bring bad luck to everybody."

CHAPTER IX

In a very handsomely furnished boudoir, Simone Desroches lay stretched upon a black divan. Standing near her was the handsome Maurice de Thouars, who was regarding her with a look in which there was more desire than pity.

"Allow me, my dear friend," said Maurice de Thouars, "to tell you that you have done wrong in sending Mlle. Bergen to Bellegarde. You know quite well that he has ceased to love you. Before you met Bellegarde you said your freedom was everything to you. Forget him." He continued: "Let me tell you again: Bellegarde was the last person for you to choose. His temperament is the reverse of yours. His love could never satisfy you. You are born to be idolized."

Thouars leant towards Simone, but, with a weak gesture, the young woman said to him : "Leave me alone, please. I know quite well that you are right, but how can I listen to you when I do not even understand my own self?"

Suddenly, a look of hope passed over Thouars's face. A little cry escaped him. Simone sat up on her divan.

Just at that moment Bellegarde alighted from the taxi, paid the driver his fare, and went to the house. Just as he rang the bell, the hunchback's motor-car stopped a few yards down the road.

The hunchback, without moving from his seat, drew a newspaper out of his pocket, which he slowly unfolded, giving the impression that he had some time to wait, and was going to pass it by reading the paper.

A chambermaid showed Jacques Bellegarde into Simone's boudoir. The latter, very excited, had laid herself down on the divan again. At the sight of Jacques, the tears which she had restrained began to flow copiously and, raising herself up from the divan, she stretched out her trembling hands towards him.

"You! You're here at last!"

"Simone," murmured Jacques, very moved by seeing her look so ill. She fell into his arms and cried: "I can't bear to think that all is finished between us!"

There was a silence, one of those painful silences – almost

tragic!

"Jacques," continued Simone, "I beg your forgiveness. I have done great wrong! I love you so! I love you too much!"

And she sighed and said: "I should have so liked to be your wife!"

"But it is impossible!" declared Bellegarde, in a compassionate but determined voice.

Simone took some letters which were on a little tray beside her. "Your dear letters," she said. She opened one of them.

Bellegarde made a gesture as if to signify that it was of no use, but Simone, in a desperate voice, read:

"We must give up the idea of it. You are rich and I am poor. I could not commit such a crime as that."

"Am I not right?" observed Jacques.

Simone put the letter back on the tray. Then she let her head fall on to his shoulder; she spoke no more but started to cry again. Bellegarde felt her heart beat against his. She stretched out for his hand timidly; as if she feared he would refuse to give it to her, she seized it and slowly squeezed it.

Overcome by a sudden pity which, for the moment, he thought was love, Jacques gave her an impulsive kiss, once again sealing the ties which he thought were broken forever – then, just as suddenly, he thought of Colette. He imagined that she was there, just near him, and that she leaned towards him and murmured: "Take care!"

And with the unconscious cruelty of a man who desired to finish an affair quickly, he exclaimed: "No, I do not wish to! I cannot!"

Simone fell back on to her cushions in a grief-stricken condition. After a short while she got up, and Bellegarde was astonished to see that she was entirely transformed. Certainly her face still showed signs of her weeping, but there was a look of resignation on it.

The reporter, troubled by this sudden change, said to himself: "What has come over her? What is she going to tell me now?"

Standing up, she said in a very calm voice: "Everything seems clear to me now. It is you who are right! I have adored you, and I adore you still. You – you thought that you loved me, when in reality you were only fascinated by me. To prolong such a state of affairs would bring about only disaster, so I think it is better that we should part!"

"Simone," Bellegarde said, "it is my turn to ask your pardon."

"I repeat to you," said the young woman, "I don't want you to do so. I only hope that you succeed brilliantly in your career – I realize now that I have only been a hindrance to you. Good-bye, Jacques; go, and be happy!"

"Good-bye, Simone," replied Bellegarde.

And taking the hand of his lover for the last time, he carried it to his lips. Simone turned away her head so that she should not see him go. When he had disappeared, without a tear, without a sign, without a complaint, she gathered up her letters, tied them up with a piece of blue ribbon and locked them away in her writing-desk – then, brusquely, she tried to get up and walk a few steps, but fell down in a dead faint on to the floor.

Just then Mlle. Bergen and Maurice de Thouars came into the room. Thouars rushed up to her, and Mile. Bergen called the domestics.

The chambermaid asked: "Shall I telephone for the doctor?"

"Yes, at once!" replied Mlle. Bergen.

But Simone stammered out weakly: "What good can a doctor do? I am broken-hearted!"

And, closing her eyes, she fell again into the arms of Elsa Bergen.

"Poor Mademoiselle!" murmured Juliette to the footman.

Maurice de Thouars angrily exclaimed: "That journalist, he is responsible for all this."

While Thouars was uttering this remark, Jacques was speeding away in a taxi – still followed by the hunchback, who seemed determined never to leave his prey.

CHAPTER X

Chantecoq was just closing up a book called *History of the Louvre*, when his servant appeared and announced Jacques Bellegarde.

Chantecoq ordered the servant to show him in.

As soon as Bellegarde appeared, Chantecoq went hurriedly towards him and after a cordial handshake, he invited him to sit down.

"First of all," said Bellegarde, "allow me to thank you again."

"For what?"

"Without you, last night, I should certainly have followed Sabarat."

"You have nothing to thank me for," replied Chantecoq, with a smile.

"Come now!" exclaimed Bellegarde.

"I knew," declared the detective, "that you were passing that night in the Room of the Barbarous Gods."

"You knew?"

"It is my business to find things out. I also knew that I had only to say one word to prevent you from doing it. I did not do it, because I was only too pleased to have a witness such as you to assist at the scene which I was able to foresee would occur." Then he added: "Have you brought the documents about which you spoke to me yesterday evening?"

"Here they are," replied Bellegarde, giving him the two letters signed by Belphegor.

Chantecoq took them and read them carefully.

"This Belphegor is very audacious," declared he in a grave tone.

"That is my opinion," said Bellegarde.

"May I keep these letters?"

"Please do," said Bellegarde.

Colette then came into the room. She wore a morning dress of elegant simplicity, and a charming clôche hat. As she went up to her father, pretending not to notice the journalist, she said gaily: "Papa, I am ready."

"Monsieur Bellegarde," said the detective, "my daughter and

my secretary."

"Mademoiselle," stammered Jacques, looking from Colette to Chantecoq.

Chantecoq then said. "You had not guessed–"

"Well..." began Bellegarde hesitantly.

But Colette, wishing to change the subject, said: "Don't you think, Monsieur Bellegarde, that my father can disguise himself wonderfully well?"

"He does it admirably," declared Bellegarde. "I do not wish to be indiscreet," he continued, "but are you not ready to go out?"

"Yes," said Chantecoq. "I want to go to the Louvre with my daughter. Will you accompany us?"

"Willingly," said Bellegarde.

About twenty minutes later their taxi stopped in the great courtyard of the Louvre. The three occupants got out, and while Bellegarde settled with the chauffeur, the mysterious hunchback stopped his car within about fifty yards of them.

The journalist rejoined the detective and his daughter, and all three went in the Palace and headed to the right, towards the staircase of the Victoire de Samothrace, which was absolutely deserted.

They climbed the staircase and stopped. Chantecoq, blessed with an excellent memory, had remembered the exact place where the Phantom had disappeared into the darkness. He said to Bellegarde:

"That is the place where our ghost disappeared, is it not?"

"I believe so," said Bellegarde.

The detective looked round him and, pointing his finger to a pillar which stood on the left behind the stairs, said: "Although Monsieur Legrand Vernet's book states to the contrary, I think that there must be a secret opening there; otherwise I cannot fathom how the thief got away."

Taking a powerful magnifying glass out of his pocket. he carefully examined the pillar. Very soon, in a somewhat disappointed voice, he declared: "It is extraordinary – the column appears to be absolutely intact – there seems to be no defect anywhere. I've tapped it all over with a steel hammer, but can find no hollow parts anywhere.

"Let us also look at the flagstones; there may even be some opening under the arch of the stairs which leads to a subterranean passage."

Chantecoq thought for a moment, and then continued: "Or, there may be a simple hiding-place which the thief discovered accidentally, in which he took refuge until everybody was out of the way."

Again the detective looked around him.

"It was on the left that he disappeared – a little this way!"

He went towards a high wall covered with a thick dark tapestry which he lifted up. Behind this was a heavy oak door which had a massive lock on it.

"This door," observed the detective, "was condemned a long time ago. See how it gives!"

And, taking a plan of the museum out of his pocket, he was just readying to study it, when the cry was heard:

"Closing time – all out!"

"Then we must finish for today," concluded Chantecoq.

They had reached the courtyard and arrived at the place where the hunchback had stationed his car – the hunchback himself did not appear to be in it! Suddenly someone called out:

"Monsieur Chantecoq! Monsieur Chantecoq!"

They turned round and Pierre Gautrais, his cap in his hand, stood before them.

'Well! My good man, what is the matter?" questioned the detective.

"I am dismissed from my work," said the keeper in a desperate tone.

Chantecoq looked Gautrais straight in the face and said: "You know what I promised you?"

"Then," exclaimed Gautrais, "you will let me work for you?"

"And also your wife," said the detective.

"We are in need of a good housekeeper," said Colette, "and I know that Marie-Jeanne is a first-rate cook."

"You can count upon her," said Gautrais. "You will be well looked after."

"Are you going to take my housekeeper away from me?" exclaimed Jacques.

"I beg your pardon," said Colette, "I was not aware–"

"Please don't apologize," replied the reporter. "I certainly think a very great deal of Marie-Jeanne, but I would not deprive you and your father of her excellent services. I will get another cook."

"Marie-Jeanne will find you one," replied Gautrais.

"We shall be very pleased to have your company at dinner one evening – you can then enjoy your late housekeeper's cooking," said Monsieur Chantecoq.

"I should be only too pleased to come," said Jacques.

After cordial handshakes, they parted. Colette, when Jacques was out of sight, said to her father: "Isn't he charming, papa?"

"Yes! As the prince of the same name!" said Chantecoq, tapping Colette's cheek, which coloured up to a pretty pink.

And, taking her father's arm, she went with him in the direction of the Carrousel.

When they had gone a little way, the bulbous head of the hunchback slowly emerged from his car, in which he had been hiding. As he watched the detective and his daughter go on their way, he murmured with a hideous smile on his face:

"I believe that Belphegor will be most pleased with me!"

CHAPTER XI

The same evening during dinner Colette noticed that her father was very quiet and thoughtful, so she did not talk to him.

The detective took from the drawer of his desk the two notes signed by Belphegor, and read them again and again very carefully.

Then, taking up his magnifying glass, he scrutinized the writing, letter by letter.

Very soon, the face of the great detective showed some surprise. Opening the drawer again, he took out the little note which Jacques Bellegarde sent him saying that he would be unable to come for the appointment at the arranged hour. He placed it beside the two notes signed by Belphegor and compared them with the aid of his glass.

When he had finished, he seemed perturbed.

"It is strange," he said, "very strange."

Colette lifted her head.

"What's the matter?" she asked.

"Come and see!"

The young girl went over to him and, showing her the three notes, Chantecoq continued:

"You see these three notes? These two have been sent by Belphegor, and this one by Jacques Bellegarde. You read all three carefully, and tell me if anything strikes you about them."

Colette obeyed.

"Well?" questioned the detective, when she had finished reading them.

"I notice that Monsieur Bellegarde's writing is very distinct and bold, and that Belphegor's is irregular and obviously disguised."

"Granted. But don't you notice anything else?"

"My God! No!"

"You compare the 'B' of Bellegarde and the 'B' of Belphegor."

Colette compared the letters.

Then her father said: "Don't you find that these two 'B's appear to have been written by the same hand?"

"Yes," replied the girl.

"That's not all," continued her father: "Look well at the

curves of the 'C's."

"They are the same."

"And those of the 'L's?"

"Just the same," said Colette.

And, suddenly, in a distressed voice, Colette exclaimed: "Father, do you suspect Monsieur Bellegarde?"

The detective was silent.

"It is impossible," protested the young girl in a firm voice. "Haven't you said yourself that the Phantom wanted to strike down Monsieur Bellegarde?"

"Absolutely,"

"Then?"

"I say nothing. I simply notice that his writing and that of Belphegor bears a striking resemblance."

With some emotion, Colette continued: "I can only imagine that Belphegor has tried to imitate Monsieur Jacques's writing. Why didn't he send typewritten notes?"

"With what aim?"

"That would have given him less chance of being found out."

"That is exactly what I wanted to tell you," exclaimed the detective.

"Then you agree with me?" said Colette.

"Entirely."

"Oh! I'm so glad!"

"I am, too," replied Chantecoq, "because this discovery will help me a great deal. This proves to us that Belphegor knows Bellegarde. It is therefore in Bellegarde's circle that I must commence my research at once."

Suddenly, one of the panes in the windows of Chantecoq's office flew into pieces, and a round pebble to which a letter was attached fell at Colette's feet.

With a bound Chantecoq ran towards the window, which he quickly threw open. The garden in front of the house was deserted, but it seemed to him that a shadowy form went quickly into the Avenue Verzy and disappeared into the darkness.

Chantecoq's first thought was to rush after this unknown person. But, on reflection, he knew it would be a waste of time, as the aggressor had by now a good start of him and no doubt he had carefully planned out a way of escape. He closed the window again and returned to Colette, who had picked up the stone and handed it to her father. Chantecoq undid the thick thread which attached the letter to the stone. He then took the letter out of the envelope and read, as follows:

"*MONSIEUR CHANTECOQ:*
This is a piece of good advice. Cease occupying yourself with me or harm will come to you and your daughter.
    BELPHEGOR."

Chantecoq exclaimed: "There – it is the height of impudence!" And he continued: "Well, we will see!"

But his eyes suddenly rested on his daughter. Immediately an expression of distress spread over his face.

"You seem disturbed," said she. "Surely the threats of Belphegor have no effect on you, do they?"

"If it were a question of myself," continued the detective, "I should only laugh at them; but where you are concerned–"

"Father – you must do your duty."

"Remember, my dear, just before your mother died she made me swear that I would take her place and look after you."

"And mother made *me* promise to look after *you*," said Colette. "Father, I'm afraid I shouldn't love you quite so much if you bowed to Belphegor's demands."

"Set your mind at ease," said the detective. "Now, thanks to you, I feel stronger than ever."

CHAPTER XII

It was night time. Outside Mlle. Desroches's house one could see only two windows which looked on to the garden that showed any light – the one on the first floor which was Simone's room, and the other on the ground floor, that of the salon, where, through the transparent curtains, one could see the figures of Elsa Bergen and Maurice de Thouars. They had just left Simone who, after passing a very bad day, had at last become drowsy.

Maurice de Thouars seemed particularly agitated. He said in an angry voice: "It is too much! I simply can't stand it!"

"Monsieur de Thouars," said the companion calmly, "will you let me give you some advice?"

Thouars shrugged his shoulders.

Mlle. Bergen continued: "If you wish to fulfil your desire, you must have patience."

"I know that I have a friend in you, and you know how I love Simone – I would even go to hell for her."

A clock struck the midnight hour. Mlle. Bergen rang for Juliette.

When the chambermaid appeared, Mlle. Bergen said: "Go and see if Mlle. Simone needs anything."

Juliette replied: "I went to her a little while ago and gave her a cup of camomile. She told me she wanted to go to sleep, and that she wasn't to be disturbed."

"Never mind, just run up again and see that she is all right," ordered Mlle. Bergen.

The chambermaid obeyed. After reaching the top of the staircase, she very softly half-opened Mlle. Desroches's door and looked in – the room was lit by single night-light.

Simone was sleeping soundly.

At that moment, a strange scene was taking place in the garden. A hunchback was to be seen lurking there, and there was also a shadow gliding towards some trees – and this shadow was the Phantom of the Louvre!

Dressed in his black shroud and hood, he went towards the

half-open window of Simone's boudoir. He cautiously opened it and, without making the slightest noise, crept inside the room. With the aid of a lantern which he held in his hand, he crept quietly toward Mlle. Desroches's writing desk, opened it with a picklock and, after a minute or two, took out the letter which Simone had put in one of the drawers. Just then he heard a voice. It was Juliette's. She had returned to Elsa Bergen and was saying: "Mlle. is sleeping soundly."

With stealthy steps the intruder went towards the window, but on his way he knocked against a piece of furniture, on which was a china vase. The latter fell to the ground, shattered, and made a terrific crash.

On hearing the noise, Maurice de Thouars, Mlle. Bergen and the chambermaid all gave a start.

"There is someone in Simone's room," said the companion, and Maurice de Thouars rushed up to the boudoir and threw open the door.

Thouars gave a yell. He had just seen a hooded figure in the act of climbing over the edge of the window.

Courageously he rushed after him, but he was not quick enough to prevent the mysterious prowler from getting away.

At the same time Mlle. Bergen and Juliette had joined Thouars. He had time to see the Phantom go all along the house. The two women cried out in terror. Thouars, taking a revolver out of his pocket, shot in the direction of the Phantom who, crossing a pathway, disappeared behind a bush in the garden.

The young man then dashed outside, leaving the two women alone. The neighbouring dogs had commenced to bark, and servants quickly appeared after being woken from their sleep by the noise.

Suddenly the door opened and Simone, in her night-gown, emerged, looking very frightened and pale. She took refuge in Mlle. Bergen's arms.

Meanwhile the servants and Thouars were searching every nook and corner of the grounds.

Simone was clutching hold of one of Mlle. Bergen's hands and one of Juliette's, repeating between shivering teeth: "Oh! the ghost! the ghost!" when suddenly her eyes fell upon her writing-desk. She took her hands away from the companion and Juliette, and rushed over to it. The drawers were half-open. On searching them, she saw that Jacques's letters were missing, and she cried out: "Jacques's letters – someone has stolen Jacques's letters!"

Mile. Bergen and the chambermaid took her in their arms and tried to pacify her.

Then Maurice de Thouars reappeared, his revolver in hand; behind him followed the chauffeur and gardener.

"Simone!" he cried he in an agonized voice. He rushed up to her, but Mlle. Bergen kept him back. And the ghost?" said Mlle. Bergen.

Maurice de Thouars gravely replied: "He has disappeared!"

PART II

CHAPTER I

It was nine o'clock in the morning. On the little balcony adjoining his house, Chantecoq was sitting in a comfortable rocking-chair quietly reading a newspaper. He raised his head as he heard footsteps coming along one of the gravel paths, and saw Pierre Gautrais coming towards him, accompanied by a man of about thirty years of age. The man had with him an assistant who held two magnificent Danish dogs on a leash.

Chantecoq got up and went towards them. Gautrais presented his companion.

"This is Monsieur Carabot, a dog-handler in the Rue St. Honoré."

"As you requested, Monsieur Chantecoq," said Carabot, "I've brought you Pandore and Vidocq, my two most intelligent dogs."

"Are they in good form?" said Chantecoq.

"You have only to look at them," said the seller in a confident voice. Then he immediately ordered his assistant to release them from the leash.

The assistant obeyed. The dog-handler indicated an open window of the house, and said simply: "Go!"

Pandore and Vidocq rushed forward, jumped over the balcony, leaped through the window and disappeared like lightning into the building.

"*La! la!*" observed Chantecoq. "I hope that they will not destroy anything belonging to me."

"You needn't be afraid," said the man; and taking a whistle out of his pocket, he blew it loudly. Immediately the dogs came rushing towards him and lay down at his feet.

"Bravo!" said the detective. with evident satisfaction.

The handler gave his assistant some orders in a low voice.

The assistant went and bent down over the air-hole of the cellar and, drawing from his pocket a metal saw, he pretended to interfere with one of the bars.

It was not even necessary for Monsieur Carabot to say the word. A look towards the dogs was sufficient for them – they rushed forward; one jumped at the assistant's throat and the other seized his leg. It was obvious that the latter could not move, unless he wanted to be devoured.

Monsieur Carabot again blew the whistle, and instantaneously the two dogs released their grasp of the assistant and came and sat down at their master's feet.

"They are marvellous," declared Chantecoq, taking a cheque-book out of his pocket. "How much do you want for them?"

"To you, Monsieur Chantecoq, the price will be three thousand francs."

Then M. Carabot added: "Yesterday I refused four thousand to an American; anyhow, I'm sure they will be in good hands with you, and also it will be good publicity for me!"

Chantecoq wrote out a cheque and handed it to M. Carabot.

"They are called Pandore and Vidocq," said M. Carabot.

On hearing their names, the two beasts pricked up their ears and wagged their tails with joy.

"Go and tell your wife to prepare them some food."

"Marie-Jeanne," explained Gautrais, "has taken a new housekeeper to see Monsieur Bellegarde, but she won't be long."

"Well, I must say *au revoir*, Monsieur Chantecoq. You can rest assured that you will be well guarded."

Colette was putting some flowers in a crystal vase which was on the detective's desk.

"Good morning, father," said Colette. Then she anxiously asked: "Any news?"

"No, nothing yet," replied the detective. "And you; you haven't been dreaming of Belphegor too much, have you?"

"I have never slept so well."

A telephone bell rang and the detective took up the receiver and listened. Evidently the communication was important, for Chantecoq showed great surprise.

And as he put the receiver up, Chantecoq said, "Belphegor is still being impudent."

"What has he done now?" questioned Colette.

"It appears that last night the Phantom of the Louvre got into Mlle. Simone Desroches's house."

"The friend of Monsieur Bellegarde?" said the young girl, her cheeks slowly losing their colour.

Without appearing to notice Colette, Chantecoq continued: "He has taken a packet of letters written by the journalist that Mlle. Desroches had locked up, during the afternoon, in a writing desk to which she alone had the key."

As if he spoke to himself, he muttered: "Why this new theft... to procure a specimen of Bellegarde's handwriting? That would be a pointless thing to do!" Then he added: "Belphegor must certainly know his writing, for he has already succeeded so well in copying many of the letters, samples of which I have in my drawer in my desk. Really! this affair gets more and more involved."

"Father," observed Colette, "are they sure that the Phantom of the Louvre committed this theft?"

"Mlle. Desroches's companion, who telephoned me just now, gave such a description of him that there can be no shadow of doubt."

"It is really extraordinary," murmured Colette, trying not to show the excited state that she was in.

"So extraordinary," said the detective, "that I am going to Mlle. Desroches's house at once."

Just as Chantecoq was saying this, the door burst open and, red as a tomato, her hat on one side, and in a very perturbed condition, Marie-Jeanne entered the room, crying: "Monsieur Chantecoq – Mademoiselle Colette!"

She fell into an armchair and Colette said: "What's the matter?"

"Monsieur Jacques was not at his house, and the caretaker told me that he had been away all night. I called at the offices of *Le Petit Parisien*, and was told that they had not seen Monsieur Jacques since yesterday evening, at about eight o'clock. I fear that some harm has come to him!"

"My God!" said Colette, as Marie-Jeanne wiped two large

tears away which were trickling down her cheeks.

Chantecoq was thoughtful.

The news of the disappearance of Bellegarde bad absolutely nonplussed him – not only because it destroyed all previous calculations that he had firmly fixed in his mind, but also because it indicated that the young reporter of *Le Petit Parisien* was not sincere in his friendship towards them.

"Father, I feel that harm has come to Monsieur Jacques."

"Calm yourself, my dear!"

Chantecoq continued: "Have you still faith in me, my child?"

"Of course I have, father."

"Well! In all frankness, I feel convinced that not only is Jacques Bellegarde alive and well, but that he will dine with us tonight. Now I must say *au revoir*, as I have to go and call at Mlle. Desroches's house." And remembering Belphegor's note that he had received the day before, he added; "Promise me that you will not leave here in my absence!"

"Yes, I promise, father."

CHAPTER II

After ordering Gautrais to watch the house very carefully during his absence, Chantecoq called on Mlle. Desroches.

He was received by Elsa Bergen and Maurice de Thouars. The latter scarcely ever left the house now. Both Elsa Bergen and Thouars gave the detective a detailed report of the previous night's events. After they had finished, Chantecoq asked: "What time was it when you saw the ghost?"

"Eleven o'clock," replied M. de Thouars.

'Could you show me the piece of furniture which contained the stolen letters?'

"Will you kindly follow me," said Mlle. Bergen.

All three left the salon and went into the boudoir. M. de Thouars led the detective towards the writing-desk, which was still open.

"Nobody has touched anything?" said M. Chantecoq.

"Nothing."

"Where exactly were the letters?"

"Only Mlle. Desroches can tell you that," replied the companion; "but I am afraid she is very ill owing to this disturbance, and I doubt if she will be in a fit state to tell you."

The detective did not insist.

He examined the writing-desk very carefully, and found that it showed no signs of having been tampered with in any way.

"It is evident," concluded the detective, "that the thief – who has not damaged the desk – must have used an extremely efficient and modern instrument, unless he succeeded in obtaining an impression of the lock; the latter would bear out my inferences, that it would be necessary to look for the culprit amongst the friends of Mlle. Desroches."

"Perhaps," observed Mlle. Bergen, "a photograph of the impression would help you?"

"No! I'm afraid it wouldn't," said the detective; "and I'll tell you why. From the description which you gave me over the telephone, the thief who came here is the same as he who visited the Louvre two nights ago."

"What! you have seen him?" exclaimed the companion and Thouars simultaneously.

"As I see you now," replied Chantecoq. And in a sharp tone the detective continued: "I noticed that not only did he hide his face under a mask, but he had his body wrapped in a kind of black shroud, and he wore some black gloves which would enable him not to betray himself with fingerprints."

"Fortunately," continued the detective, "we have at our disposal other means of investigation which we can avail ourselves of–" He stopped, reflected a moment or two, and then asked: "Where was the Phantom when you saw him?"

"He was in the act of climbing out of the window here," replied M. de Thouars.

"It is exceedingly curious!" said Chantecoq. After a brief silence, he asked: "May I also explore the garden?"

"Certainly," said M. de Thouars; "and I will be your guide."

"You are very kind."

Chantecoq studied the ground very carefully – there appeared to be no sign of any footprints – the branches revealed no breakage, and the leaves did not seem to have been bruised at all. He therefore came to the conclusion that Belphegor had not hidden there. Chantecoq said nothing of this to Thouars. They then went all over the garden and came down by the wall which enclosed the house.

The surface of the wall was absolutely smooth – there was no trellis work covering it, it was freshly painted, and bore no marks showing that anyone had scaled it. The trees in the grounds were not near enough to the wall to be an aid to anyone to climb over; moreover, there was a jagged covering of broken glass on the top of the wall.

Still silent, Chantecoq, followed by Thouars, walked along the whole length of the wall – by which there was a flower-bed – but nothing appeared to have been disturbed there either.

Suddenly Chantecoq stopped. He found that he was in front of a little door which was painted in a dark green shade, the lock of which was covered with rust marks.

"Where does this lead to?" asked Chantecoq.

"To a little street," replied M. de Thouars, "which is called, I believe, Lilac Road."

Chantecoq tried the latch – the door did not move.

"The door has been unused for a long time," declared Thouars.

They went on and came to a very high building of one storey, the architecture of which was very bizarre and ultra-modern. On seeing it, Chantecoq asked: "What is that?"

"The studio of Mlle. Desroches," said Maurice de Thouars.

They went right up to it, and Thouars opened the door so that Chantecoq could see inside.

After looking carefully round the studio, Chantecoq said suddenly in an interested tone: "Who can say if the Phantom has not succeeded in hiding himself under one of these couches, or even in one of these huge chests?"

"It is impossible," said M. de Thouars. "At night the door of this studio is always locked, so he couldn't possibly take refuge there. However, Monsieur Chantecoq, if you wish to see–"

"Don't bother," said the detective and, giving a peculiar smile, he said: "It is necessary to ask one's self whether Belphegor has wings or not." Then he added: "May I again examine Mlle. Desroches's writing-desk?"

"Certainly, Monsieur Chantecoq."

Chantecoq and Thouars then returned to the salon, where Mlle. Bergen awaited them.

Chantecoq went to examine the writing-desk, and with the aid of his magnifying-glass he looked carefully at the lock; he wanted to see if the thief had used a skeleton key or a special pick-lock.

"Well?" asked Mlle. Bergen of M. de Thouars in a low voice.

"He hasn't discovered anything," replied Thouars. "I am surprised. He appeared to be rather embarrassed!"

The companion was just going to speak to Thouars when she suddenly saw Simone come into the room.

"Simone," she said, "This is most unwise!"

On hearing these words, the detective turned his head.

Simone looked very pale. She was wearing a translucent night-gown, and came forward with a hesitant step, leaning on the arm of her chambermaid.

"Monsieur Chantecoq," she said, in a weak voice, "I knew you were here." And, forcing a smile, she added: "Have you made any interesting discovery?"

"Nothing definite yet," replied the king of the detectives. "But if it does not tire you too much, perhaps you will kindly give me some information?"

"Ask me anything you wish, Monsieur Chantecoq."

"Did the Phantom steal some of your letters?"

"Yes."

"Some intimate letters?"

"Some intimate ones."

"Anything else?"

"No, Monsieur."

"You are quite sure of it?"

"Absolutely sure."

"These letters, from what Mlle. Bergen told me over the telephone, were those of Jacques Bellegarde?"

"Yes, Monsieur."

"Thank you, Mademoiselle, for the information."

Simone still appeared to be very upset. She took the detective by the hand and implored him not to leave her.

"Simone, I beg of you, calm yourself," advised Elsa Bergen.

"We are here to look after you," exclaimed M, de Thouars.

"Have no fear, Mademoiselle," said Chantecoq, "I am certain that the Phantom will never appear in your house again."

"Nevertheless," objected Simone in a trembling voice, "he visited the Louvre on two consecutive nights."

The detective replied:

"He did so, it's true – but only because, on his first visit, he did not attain his goal; while here–"

"While here?" said Simone.

"He has taken all that he wanted," replied Chantecoq.

"Jacques's letters," said the young woman.

With trembling lips, she continued: "That is exactly what frightens me. The Phantom certainly wants to use these letters against him – for revenge. It is dreadful!"

"Jacques Bellegarde is well able to look after himself," replied Chantecoq.

Simone continued: "Listen to me, Monsieur Chantecoq. What I have to tell you is very serious; it may throw some light on this gloomy affair."

She continued: "About forty-eight hours ago I received a note signed by Belphegor, which threatened Jacques with the most terrible calamities if he persisted in interfering in this Louvre affair.

"You understand me, don't you?" she continued. "If the thief is not caught, I simply can't live–"

Chantecoq looked down at her and thought to himself, *Poor woman! how highly-strung!*

Then in a loud voice he continued: "Mademoiselle, you can rely upon me – I already know Monsieur Bellegarde – we are on quite friendly terms."

"Thank you!" stammered Mlle. Desroches, closing her eyes and letting her head fall on to one of the cushions on the couch.

Chantecoq was just about to take his departure when the young woman's companion called him aside and said:

"Monsieur Chantecoq, may we inform the police now?"

Chantecoq thought for a few seconds, then said gravely:

"Not yet."

"Very well, Monsieur Chantecoq, we will keep silent for as long as you deem it necessary."

CHAPTER III

It was four o'clock in the afternoon.

The detective went into the house, hung up his hat and coat, and sat down at his desk. He opened the drawer which contained Belphegor's notes, and also the one that jacques had sent, and placed them before him. Then, taking hold of his magnifying glass, he examined the documents again.

"It is extraordinary," he murmured. "The more one compares them, the more one has the impression that certain characteristics have been written by the same hand. Nevertheless, I feel sure that Jacques Bellegarde cannot be the Phantom of the Louvre, as the latter has attempted to assassinate him twice. This Belphegor is certainly the sharpest forger of my acquaintance!"

A sound of footsteps was heard in the room. It was Colette. In a tremulous voice she said: "Father, have you learnt anything of interest?"

"The information which I have obtained at Mlle. Desroches's house has convinced me more than ever that Belphegor wants to throw the blame on Jacques Bellegarde for the misdeeds which he has committed."

"Then," said the young girl nervously, "my presentiments have a foundation."

"Colette!" reproached the detective firmly, "I don't seem to recognize you these days – you appear to have lost all your self-control." Then he added: "As to Jacques Bellegarde, I don't think it will be long before we see him again."

"Provided that Belphegor has not killed him, as he did the keeper, Sabarat," said Colette.

"I would stake my life that he is alive," said Chantecoq.

Scarcely had Chantecoq said these words, than he heard his dogs begin to bark. He got up and went to the window.

"Heavens!" said the detective, "I was right. Here is Monsieur Bellegarde!"

Colette, suddenly becoming joyful, joined her father at the window.

Gautrais, after quietening the dogs, accompanied the reporter to the house. Chantecoq welcomed him at the door of his office.

On seeing Bellegarde's pale and drawn face, Chantecoq said: "Where have you been?"

Bellegarde replied:

"I have just managed to escape being assassinated."

Then he continued: "I was at the offices of *Le Petit Parisien* yesterday, correcting some proofs of my article, when the telephone rang. On answering it, I was informed that my friend Dermont – who is, by the way, a celebrated painter – was very seriously ill.

Imagine my surprise! I had met him the day before in the Boulevard Montmartre, and he then appeared to be in perfect health. The person who telephoned me, one of his neighbours, said that Dermont had been knocked down during the day, and was suffering from concussion of the brain and had not gained consciousness. On hearing this, I did not hesitate to take the train to Nesles-la-Vallee, where Dermont lives on a charming estate – I have had some very enjoyable times there with him. Two hours later, I reached Nesles Station."

"What time was it?" interrupted the detective.

"About eleven o'clock."

"Very well! Continue," said Chantecoq.

The reporter continued: "I started out to walk to my friend's house. It was a dark night, and on either side of the road were great bushes. After walking about three hundred yards, I saw a car standing near a heap of debris. It was a dark-coloured car. A mechanic, dressed in overalls, who had a black moustache and was wearing a cyclist's cap well down over his eyes was, with the aid of a lamp, examining one of the back wheels of the car. On hearing the sound of my footsteps, he turned round and called out to me: 'Can you give me a hand?' I approached him, and he said: 'I think that something has gone wrong with my car. It is most annoying!'

"I leant over him in order to help, when all of a sudden I received a terrific blow with a bludgeon on the nape of my neck which literally stunned me, and I lost consciousness. When I came to, I was lying in the car, which was travelling at full speed. Someone whose face I could hardly see was holding me down. I saw that he was a hunchback and that he held a revolver in his hand, which showed me clearly that he was ready to send me to the netherworld if I showed any signs of struggling."

Bellegarde continued: "I remained quite still and closed my eyes. Some minutes later the car stopped on a bridge over the River Oise. The chauffeur got out of his seat, opened the carriage door, then taking hold of my legs, with the hunchback at the same time taking me by the shoulders, they dragged me out of the car. Holding my breath, and keeping as still as a corpse, I said to myself: 'They are certainly going to throw me into the Oise – and that will just suit me well, because I'm a first-rate swimmer!'"

At that point, Colette could not suppress a terror-stricken cry. Jacques Bellegarde looked at her tenderly; but Chantecoq, with a sign, ordered the journalist to continue.

Bellegarde continued immediately: "What I had anticipated was correct. Both of them, without the least hesitation on their part, and without the least resistance on mine, threw me over the bridge into the river in the middle of a backwater. The night was dark... I swam and hid myself behind a huge buttress of the bridge, in order to let my assassins think that I had disappeared.

"My ruse succeeded. Five minutes later – which seemed to me to be as long as a century – during which time the hunchback and chauffeur were having a good look in order to assure themselves that I had not come to the surface, I heard the roar of the car's engine – it sounded as if the car was being driven off in the direction of Paris. I was saved!

"I then swam towards the bank. When I reached it, I almost fainted. It was daylight when I came to, and I felt just as if I had been awakened out of a heavy sleep. I took the first train to Paris and, without even going home, I came direct to see you, because I wanted to inform you of my misadventure."

"My daughter and I began to feel uneasy about you," declared the detective.

"You see, father," observed Colette, "that I was not far wrong."

"As to myself," said Chantecoq, with a smile, "I must say I felt very puzzled once or twice."

"Belphegor has kept to his promise," said the reporter, 'because I feel certain that it was he who struck me down."

"Say rather that he wished to assassinate you," replied Chantecoq.

"Then," exclaimed Bellegarde, "you think that it was not he who gave me the blow?"

"It was impossible! At the precise moment when you arrived at Nesles-la-Vallee, Belphegor was at Mlle. Desroches's house.

"Would you mind examining these letters very carefully?"

Jacques did so, and after a moment or two Chantecoq continued:

'Don't you notice anything strange about them?"

"No, I don't," said Jacques.

"Don't you think that there is a similarity between Belphegor's writing and your own?"

"At first sight, I did not notice it – but I see now that you are quite right." And, looking at the detective, he added: "And you infer–?"

Chantecoq said: "I conclude that Belphegor has bidden his accomplices to do that foul trick so that he can cast suspicion on you."

The reporter exclaimed: "But that's abominable!"

Very quietly the king of the detectives said: "On the contrary, I think it is splendid."

Chantecoq continued: "Listen to me. You must agree with me that we are at last beginning to see daylight. Now, aren't we certain of two things? The first is that Belphegor is not an isolated criminal, and that he has accomplices ready to do all the things which he orders them to do.

"Well, then!" added Chantecoq, "haven't we also proof that Belphegor is trying to masquerade as yourself?"

"Granted!" said Jacques. "So what do you want me to do?"

Chantecoq brusquely replied: "Disappear."

"Disappear?" exclaimed Bellegarde. "It's impossible! It's–"

The detective interrupted: "Or rather live here, unknown to everyone, which will allow me to set a trap for Belphegor in my own fashion – a trap into which he cannot fail to fall."

"Monsieur Chantecoq," said Bellegarde, "for some time I

have admired you, but now that I know you intimately, I have absolute confidence in you and I should be only too pleased to help you in this affair, which I feel sure will have sensational results. Of course, I quite see that if you wish to lure Belphegor into a trap, it will be better that he believes me to be dead."

"Then you agree," said the detective.

"Excuse me, I've not finished," declared Bellegarde. "Unfortunately, I've no near relatives, but I have many good friends, I'm pleased to say. And there is my newspaper–"

Chantecoq objected: "You will receive warmest congratulations from your Chief."

"I must have time to think."

Chantecoq slowly raised his eyebrows and looked at his daughter. Then, suddenly, someone knocked on the door.

"Come in," said the detective.

Marie-Jeanne appeared with a parcel in her hand and said: "A messenger has just delivered this for Mlle. Colette."

Colette untied the parcel. It was a beautiful box of chocolates. With a smile, she said to Bellegarde:

"Monsieur Bellegarde, you spoil me!"

The journalist looked surprised and said: "Mademoiselle, you are mistaken. I haven't sent you this present."

"But here is your card," insisted the detective's daughter. Colette then showed Bellegarde the card, on which was clearly engraved his own name and address.

More and more puzzled, the reporter said: "Mademoiselle, I give you my word of honour that I did not send you these chocolates, even although this card appears to be identical to those I use."

The situation was clear to Chantecoq, and he said: "Ah! this is the work of Belphegor!"

Chantecoq took hold of the box and asked Colette and Bellegarde to follow him. He went to the far end of his office and opened a little door, through which they passed. They were in a small, well-lit room – Chantecoq's laboratory.

"It has no suspicious smell about it," he declared, "However, I will bet–"

Chantecoq got up and went towards a cupboard which

contained many pharmaceutical bottles of all sizes, each bearing a label giving the name of the liquid it contained.

The detective took hold of one of these, returned to the table, poured about half the contents of it into one of the smallest test-tubes, and then threw a piece of broken chocolate into it.

Jacques and Colette looked on in silence.

At the end of a few moments Chantecoq took hold of the test-tube, held it up to the light and looked at it. The sweet substance gradually dissolved, and numerous brown-coloured globules settled to the bottom of the tube, forming a greyish sediment, separating themselves from the other products of which the chocolate was composed.

Chantecoq declared in a trembling voice: "Now, I am certain of it; these candies are poisoned."

Colette went pale and Bellegarde exclaimed: "The thief has kept his promise – after me, you and your daughter. What a filthy trick to do – it's outrageous!" Then he added angrily: "Belphegor will stop at nothing to achieve his aims."

"This thief planned out his plot very well," said Chantecoq. "After disposing of you, he wished to get rid of Colette and I, and to lay the suspicion of his crimes on you.

"Well, what is your decision?"

The reporter answered: "I think you are right – I had better disappear!"

"Good," said Chantecoq, gripping him by the hand.

CHAPTER IV

Chantecoq had not been successful in capturing Belphegor, but at least he had discovered a few things about his adversary – he was not working entirely in the dark; whereas Inspector Menardier, in spite of all his endeavours, had found out nothing at all.

Menardier gave orders that excavations were to be made in the interior of the museum. Detectives were instructed to watch suspicious persons, but not one of them was able to find anybody who could be accused of being the Phantom of the Louvre.

The police officers were very puzzled about it all, and the public began to get unnerved; several newspapers had already severely criticized the efficiency of the police in the matter.

Monsieur Ferval had a private talk with Menardier in order to see if, between them, they couldn't throw some light on the affair.

"Monsieur Ferval," declared Menardier, "we have not discovered anything, but in this we are not alone. There is our friend Chantecoq. I've heard from a good source that he himself is very perplexed. The more I rack my brain, the more I say that for the Phantom to return on two consecutive nights to the Room of the Barbarous Gods, and not to hesitate in murdering Sabarat, clearly shows that he had some very strong motive – not merely a desire to steal a valuable object."

"Well!" said M. Ferval. "That's just what enrages me."

Menardier replied: "I have often been ordered to investigate affairs out in the East, and whilst there I saw for myself that there existed many secret societies. They were extremely powerful and had branches everywhere."

"We know that," said M. Ferval.

"That is why," declared Menardier, "I wondered if the statue of Belphegor might not serve as a hiding-place used by one of these numerous societies."

"My dear Menardier, what you are suggesting to me is only suitable for one of Pierre Benoit's novels. It is very thrilling and, no doubt, the great popular novelist would make a very good tale out of it, but a detective such as you must not be so imaginative; besides, you have already stated that the statue of Belphegor was an entirely massive block of stone."

That's true," said Menardier, "but I've since thought that it might have a secret structure inside it."

"Come now! clever and shrewd as you are, if this structure existed, you would have already discovered it."

"I'm not so sure of that," said Menardier. "But I intend to set a trap for him in the Room of the Barbarous Gods one of these nights. And yet, he must realise by now that we are on his trail, so he probably won't dare to appear again!"

"Yes, he will, if we can put him on the wrong track," said M. Ferval.

"Perhaps—"

"Wait a moment," said M. Ferval; and he scribbled the following lines, which he afterwards read over to Menardier:

"*We have learned that Inspector Menardier, who was ordered to investigate the Louvre affair, has departed today on a confidential mission to an unknown destination.*

"*The Phantom of the Louvre, finding it impossible to cross the border, may be taking refuge in a little village in the north, where no doubt he will soon be captured.*

"*We will say no more, so that we don't interfere with the police's strategy. Let us therefore wait for some further revelations, which will surely not be long in coming to light.*"

When he had finished reading the above, he continued: "I am going to send this note to the Press immediately, so that it appears in the third edition of the evening papers."

Then he added: "You will remain quietly here in a room at the back of my office, where your dinner will be brought to you. Then about ten o'clock, you will go to the Louvre with two detectives whom you may choose yourself. You will hide yourselves in the room in question and if, as I hope, the Phantom is duped by our communication and returns to the Louvre, then this time he won't escape you."

"No, Monsieur, he certainly won't," said Menardier. "And I

hope that we shan't have need to use our revolvers, and that we bring him back alive."

"If you do that, my dear Menardier," concluded M. Ferval, "you will be the one to be called 'King of the Detectives', and not Chantecoq,"

Obeying his superior's orders, Menardier went to the Louvre with his two men, and in accordance with their instructions, they hid behind two large statues in the Room of the Barbarous Gods, with Menardier in an enormous basin where he entirely disappeared from sight.

Through the large barred windows which looked out on to the courtyard of the Louvre, the moon was shining on the head of the black god Belphegor, and falling at the foot of the pedestal, on the mosaic flagstones which were stained by the blood of the keeper, Sabarat.

At the same hour, a strange scene was taking place inside the Saint-Germain-l'Auxerrois Church, which stood in front of the celebrated column of Perrault.

In the middle of the chancel, a little lamp, the red light of which must never be extinguished, shone in front of the altar. All of a sudden, the door of a confessional slowly opened. A shadowy figure emerged, then another. They were the hunchback and the mechanic in the overalls!

The mechanic carried a large portmanteau in his hand: they both glided quietly behind the altar. They stayed there for a moment and listened. No noise was heard. The hunchback then took out of his pocket an electric lamp and, switching it on, he pointed it towards the ground.

He knelt down and touched a flagstone, in the centre of which one could still faintly perceive the outline of a *fleur-de-lys*, which had been sculptured in the granite many centuries ago.

Slowly the flagstone displaced itself, showing a large hole, and then a narrow stone staircase. The hunchback and his companion went in, and as soon as they were inside the flagstone closed back into its place. After descending about forty steps, the two men reached a corridor, the roof and walls of which were forged from heavy stonework. The ground had many cracks in it, through which the river

Seine slightly percolated owing to its proximity. As they went along, enormous rats scampered about. After they had gone about a hundred yards, they stopped in front of a massive oak door which was ornamented with great rusty iron bindings in the form of a shamrock.

The hunchback knocked three times.

The door half-opened, and the two accomplices passed through it into a kind of crypt in the form of a rotunda.

A lantern hung on the wall, and its light shone on a sinister human figure sitting on a throne.

It was the Phantom of the Louvre!

The figure's body was draped in a black shroud, and its head was hidden by its hood – it seemed to be waiting for the hunchback and the mechanic who, a moment or two later, approached it respectfully.

The mechanic put down the portmanteau at the Phantom's feet. The hunchback, at the same time, held the electric lamp and withdrew from the bag a tube of the dimension of those air-pumps which are used to inflate motor-car tyres.

Then the hunchback spoke in a low voice to the Phantom, who listened attentively and approved by raising his head.

Then, after replacing the tube in the portmanteau, the hunchback got up and said: "This time, O Belphegor, the victory is ours!"

The Phantom removed the air tube from the portmanteau, where the hunchback had just put it, and slipped it under his shroud. He went towards the door and opened it wide.

Preceded by the hunchback, who had reignited his electric lamp, and followed by the mechanic, he strode silently towards the Louvre.

Belphegor and his two accomplices, after walking about a hundred and fifty yards, arrived before a staircase exactly corresponding to that which the secret opening revealed behind the altar of Saint-Germain-l'Auxerrois. They noiselessly ascended it and found themselves in front of a wall.

The Phantom laid his finger on the centre of a small stone in the wall, which slowly rose out of it. The wall then half-opened without the least noise, showing a large aperture, through which

Belphegor, the mechanic and the hunchback passed; they emerged on the landing of the Victoire de Samothrace – the same place where Chantecoq and Bellegarde had previously seen the Phantom disappear.

The three of them descended the stairs and reached the landing below. Belphegor then made a sign to the hunchback to extinguish his lamp, and alone he went into a dark corridor.

Creeping along, he reached the entrance to the Room of the Barbarous Gods and, standing still, he put the instrument which he held hidden under his shroud on the ground.

He knelt down and unscrewed the top of the air-pump, thereby allowing the somniferous gas which it contained to escape. He pointed the tube in the direction of Menardier and his two men; then, getting up again, he waited – motionless and invisible.

From the bottom of the basin where he was lying Menardier – who, by the way, had very acute hearing – detected a slight sound, and raised himself up to peer around him.

It seemed to him as if one of the detectives who was hidden behind a statue tottered, as though he had become suddenly giddy.

Menardier noticed that he began to feel a little light-headed himself. He got up out of the basin, and at the same time, his colleague fell down on to the flagstones. With cloudy head, shaking legs, and feeling half-suffocated, Menardier approached him.

Just then the other detective came staggering out of his hiding-place. On seeing him, Menardier managed to seize him by the arm, but the man slipped down on to the ground at the side of his colleague.

Gradually feeling worse, the detective endeavoured to walk a few steps; but suddenly he stopped. A terrifying spectre was coming slowly towards him through the darkness.

Menardier mechanically put his hand towards his revolver, which was in one of his pockets, but he had not the time to grasp it... the Phantom was near him, holding a bludgeon in his hand.

Gathering up his last strength, which seemed about to leave him at any minute, the detective seized Belphegor's threatening arm, and, at the same time, he tilted up the hood which entirely concealed his face.

A cry escaped him.

The mysterious thief was wearing a mask to protect him against the sleeping-gas.

Darting backwards, the Phantom pulled out of Menardier's grasp.

Menardier tried to seize hold of him again, but he collapsed, in a dead faint, on to the ground just by the inert bodies of his two colleagues.

Belphegor then leant over the three men in turn and, certain that they would be unconscious for some time, he whistled.

The hunchback and the mechanic appeared. Both of them wore a mask similar to that of Belphegor.

The three intruders crept up to the statue of the demon Belphegor, which was still standing in the same place. They did not stay there long. On a sign from the Phantom, the two assistants took hold of the pedestal of the statue, and, not without effort, they skilfully and silently turned it sideways in order to uncover the part of the flagstone on which it rested.

During this operation the Phantom remained motionless, with his eyes riveted on Menardier and his colleagues, who appeared to be as rigid as the marble and stone images which loomed over them.

It was only when the pedestal was pushed aside and the piece of ground which it covered could be seen, that the flesh-and-blood Belphegor turned his head away from the three detectives.

The Phantom examined the ground while the hunchback stood over him with the lamp. In the centre of a flagstone there was another *fleur-de-lys*. This represented the arms of the Valois, and the Phantom pressed it firmly with his black-gloved fingers.

Slowly and noiselessly the flagstone moved, showing a large hole at the bottom of which lay a voluminous chest. Then the Phantom made a sign to the two accomplices, and they stretched themselves out on the ground, one on each side of the hole, into which they both put an arm.

Their hands met and seized the metal handles fixed at the two ends of the heavy chest. They pulled the chest out, with great difficulty, and placed it near the statue, which was turned upside down.

The Phantom examined the chest.

On the lid, which was made of Cordova leather, some royal

arms were faintly to be seen, above which one could just decipher the initials of Henry III, King of France.

One of the four iron bindings which surrounded the corners of the chest was nearly detached. Belphegor pulled it off entirely and examined it. Then, without saying a word, he pointed to the door of the room.

The two men carried the chest on their shoulders, the weight of which made them stoop a little.

After throwing the iron binding down on the ground, the Phantom, with the lamp in his hand, went towards the corridor, followed by his two accomplices.

The hunchback picked up the air pump, which lay at the entrance to the door. All three then ascended the staircase of the Victoire de Samothrace and reached the landing.

Belphegor again performed the necessary operation to open the secret entrance. Some minutes later, they entered the crypt of the church.

The mechanic in the filthy overalls, who was perspiring heavily, laid the chest on the ground. The hunchback and he took off their masks. Then the mechanic, without losing a moment, turned the three locks with the aid of a cold chisel which he had taken out of one of his pockets. He opened the lid.

The hunchback immediately held his electric lamp over the box, and Belphegor – who was in front of him – could not suppress an exclamation of surprise; a cry of victory!

The chest was filled with magnificent jewels and pieces of gold!

The mechanic put his hand in the box and brought out a fistful of coins, which were marked with the effigy of King Henry III. As he put them back again into the box the hunchback, in his turn, took out a most magnificent crown set with precious stones.

"The diadem of Catherine of the Medicis," he murmured, drooling, and showing it admiringly to the Phantom.

The Phantom then whispered some words to the hunchback, and the latter replaced the crown in the box and with a knife tried to move one of the iron bindings; but he could not.

At the same hour, Simone Desroches was lying half-naked in her bed, appearing to be in a deep sleep. Her face looked very pale – nearly bloodless.

After Chantecoq's visit to her, she had been stricken with a violent fit of choking, and everybody felt convinced she was going to die. When the choking had subsided, she fell prostrate and had to be carried to her bed.

Distracted, Maurice de Thouars decided to go for the doctor, but just as he was going Simone came to her senses and declared that she did not wish to see a physician.

Elsa Bergen tried to insist on the doctor coming, but Simone was stubborn and would not give way; she looked at them both with an expression on her face which seemed to say: "I feel that everything is finished... let me die here in peace!" After that, she fainted.

Her companion did not leave Simone for a moment. Towards eight o'clock she seemed a little better – she breathed more freely and her lips had lost the violet tinge which had worried Elsa Bergen.

Mlle. Bergen told Juliette to inform all the servants of Simone's serious state of health, and to ask them to move about the house very quietly.

Towards midnight, the companion rang for Juliette again. She crept softly towards the door to opened it for her and said in a low whisper: "It seems as though she is a little better now; anyhow, she is very quiet; you go to bed now and I will stay with her."

Juliette was very devoted to her mistress and wished to stay with her; however, after a great deal of persuasion from the companion, she went to bed.

Mlle. Bergen locked the door, and was sitting down on a chair near Simone's bed when the clock of a neighbouring church slowly sounded the midnight hour.

An hour later, the car of the bow-legged hunchback was to be seen parked in the Avenue d'Antin, a few houses down from Jacques Bellegarde's residence. But this time it was the mechanic who was sitting in the front seat. From time to time the latter looked towards the young reporter's abode. It was clear that he was waiting for someone. That someone was none other than the hunchback, who was occupied on some sinister business.

After breaking into the journalist's apartment, with the aid of a full set of skeleton keys, the hunchback went into his office, the windows of which were sealed with the curtains drawn.

When he had closed and bolted the door he turned on the electric light, extinguished his torch which he put on the table and, after looking carefully round the room, he went up to the bookcase.

Taking hold of a few of the books which were in the middle of the centre shelf, and putting them under his left arm, he felt in one of the pockets of his overcoat and took out an object which he quickly put at the back of the shelf from where he had taken the books; he then replaced the books on the shelf.

Going up to Bellegarde's desk, he selected with an experienced eye one of the keys from his bunch and without the slightest difficulty opened up one of the drawers. He placed a bundle of letters inside the drawer, along with the iron binding belonging to the old treasure-chest, which he took out of one of his other pockets. He carefully closed the drawer, relit his lamp, extinguished the electric light, went into the ante-room, and from thence crept into the lobby; he turned the key of the door and went to the hall-porter's box and said to the porter: "Open the door, please!"

A click, and the hunchback found himself in the street. He quickly rejoined his colleague, and they drove away into the night.

CHAPTER V

The first rays of dawn filtered across the roofs of the Louvre.

Very soon the day-keepers of the museum arrived, thus liberating their colleagues who had been on duty during the night, and who – under the instructions of the Management and of Menardier – had kept a careful watch on the Room of the Barbarous Gods.

"Anything happened?" questioned the day-keepers.

"No! Nothing!" declared the night-keepers. One of them said, voicing the opinion of all the others: "It's all over now! If we want to lock up Sabarat's assassin it is no use to look here for him, I am sure that he must be far away by now!"

Pierre Gautrais's successor, a young man named Albert Droquin, who had been with the management for only a few months, went into the gallery of the Antiques, together with another senior keeper named Father Bizot; the latter was ordered to guard the statue of Venus de Milo and the other marvellous sculptures which surrounded it.

Droquin, who was usually very outgoing and communicative, seemed to be quite the reverse on this day.

"What's the matter with you?" grumbled Father Bizot, looking at his colleague with a jeering glance.

"Nothing, Father Bizot!"

"Have you got a headache? Anyone would think you'd been at war with the devil himself."

"No! indeed!" replied Droquin.

"Well! what is it? Are you unhappily married, or what?" said Father Bizot.

Then Father Bizot added: "Come now, be frank! There must be a reason. You're frightened to find yourself where the ghost has visited. Is that it?"

"No, I'm not," protested Droquin. "Only–"

"Only what?"

"Well! Each time that I come on duty I tremble in spite of myself; it seems to me just as though I see our poor Sabarat dying at the foot of the statue, and weakly crying out: 'The ghost! the ghost!'"

Then Droquin added: "And I say–"

Droquin stopped, then he said: "Father Bizot, don't you notice a funny odour?"

The old keeper sniffed into the air and said: "Heavens, no!"

"I assure you that if... anyone would think that a bottle of chloroform had been spilt." And looking around the Room of the Barbarous Gods, he shouted out: "What's that?"

He saw Menardier and his two colleagues lying inanimate on the ground. just where Belphegor and his accomplices had left them.

"Father Bizot!" shouted Droquin, "Father Bizot, look there!"

They both moved nervously towards Menardier, whom they immediately recognized. They found that the Inspector and his two officers were still breathing.

The old keeper told Droquin to go and inform the Curator as quickly as he could.

When Droquin had gone, Father Bizot leant towards Menardier, who seemed to be half-waking. Several other keepers, who had been attracted by the noise, then rushed into the room. Some went and looked at the three detectives; others stopped dead in front of the large hole where the pedestal of Belphegor's statue had been.

"The thief!" said one.

"The wretch!" said another.

"This time he has three victims!" said another.

"No!" said Father Bizot, who was the only calm one amongst them. "Don't you see that they are still living?"

Menardier and his two men were indeed beginning to show signs of life, and when M. Lavergne, the Curator, and M. Rabusson, his assistant, arrived with Droquin, Menardier was half opening his eyes. Aided by two keepers, he got up, looking very dazed. Several times he passed his hand over his forehead, saying:

"It is ridiculous! I must have been dreaming!"

After looking at the two other detectives, who had also gradually come to, M. Lavergne approached Menardier and said to him:

"What has happened?"

"Ah! it's you, Monsieur!" said Menardier in a sleepy voice.

"Yes! my friend, try and pull yourself together and tell me–"

"Monsieur, you couldn't imagine it!" said Menardier.

"Ah! you've seen the Phantom?"

"Yes! Monsieur! and I swear by the heavens above that I thought my last hour had actually come!"

While everybody was listening to Menardier, an immaculately-dressed, elderly man, wearing a grey felt hat well-drawn down over his eyes, entered the room.

It was Chantecoq.

Noticing that everyone was occupied with Menardier, he looked round the room and his eye fell upon the large hole out of which Belphegor and his accomplices had hauled the chest containing the Valois treasures. Then he noticed the iron binding which had been thrown down by the Phantom, and which lay quite near to the hole.

The detective bent down and picked up the clasp.

At that moment Menardier was saying: "It is fortunate that the thief did not murder all three of us."

There was a murmur of sympathy from everyone.

Then Menardier continued: "In my career as a detective, I have never been mixed up in such an extraordinary drama. I wonder whatever will come next?"

A resonant voice was then heard: "I'm just about to tell you, my dear friend."

Everyone looked up and, to their surprise, they saw Chantecoq standing before them.

On seeing the great detective, Monsieur Menardier frowned and said dryly: "Well, what is he interfering for?"

Chantecoq noticed the hostile reception that Menardier gave him and, without getting annoyed, he pointed in the direction of the large hole and said in a calm voice: "There has been a treasure hidden there!"

"A treasure?" repeated Menardier in an incredulous voice.

"Certainly!" said the great detective. "A treasure enclosed in a Renaissance chest."

"But what makes you think that?"

"This iron binding which I have just picked up near that hole."

Chantecoq showed the binding to M. Lavergne and added: "I

think, Monsieur, that I am not mistaken!"

"Indeed! said M. Lavergne, "this piece of ironwork dates back to the 16th century."

"Allow me to point out to you that it bears the Valois arms," continued the great detective.

Menardier said in a mistrusting and almost aggressive voice: "It is only a supposition."

"Which is confirmed," said the king of the detectives, "by the fact that the Phantom put you and your colleagues to sleep with the aid of sleeping-gas."

At these words Menardier looked distinctly displeased. And Chantecoq, patting him familiarly on the shoulder, added: "Don't you think it fortunate that the Phantom did not use poison gas?"

Menardier bit his lip.

A messenger appeared, carrying a letter addressed to Menardier. The latter opened it with a trembling hand. As he read the contents, an expression of joy and almost of triumph passed over his face. And in a self-assured, and somewhat defiant tone of voice, he said to Chantecoq: "Monsieur Chantecoq, if you will kindly be at the quay Orfevres at about five o'clock this afternoon, I think I shall have some good news for you."

The king of detectives quietly replied: "I shall be there, my dear friend."

Menardier, addressing M. Lavergne and his assistant, said: "Messieurs, I think I can safely say that it will not now be long before the Phantom is in our clutches."

And turning towards Chantecoq, who had not appeared to be at all interested in his remark, he said to him in an ironic voice: "You see, Police Headquarters still know how to go about their work."

"I have no doubt about it, my dear Menardier," replied Chantecoq in a polite tone of voice.

"Then, so long, Monsieur Chantecoq!"

"So long, my dear Menardier!"

Menardier then went away with his two colleagues.

Chantecoq slipped the iron clasp which he held in his hand into his pocket.

CHAPTER VI

In the large salon of Simone Desroches's house, Elsa Bergen and Maurice de Thouars were receiving several friends, who – having learnt that Simone was very seriously ill – had hastened to see her.

The companion, looking very desolate, was talking to two aesthetes, who were listening to the bad news which she had to tell them. Maurice de Thouars was speaking to a young female artist.

"Will you allow me to go and see her – just for a minute, no longer – merely to kiss her?" said the painter.

"It is impossible, Mademoiselle. The doctor will allow no one to see her. He will scarcely allow me to, and with the exception of two nurses, who wait on her, nobody is allowed to go into her room."

"Then, I shall go. *Au revoir*, Mademoiselle!"

"*Au revoir.*"

And the young artist left, looking so very forlorn that one would have thought that she was already following Simone's hearse.

The two aesthetes also made their departure. A few minutes later the footman announced: "Baron and Baroness Papillon."

The Baroness did not give Elsa Bergen time to greet her; she rushed into the room, and said in a tearful voice:

"Your telephone is out of order!"

Baron Papillon approached Elsa Bergen with a vacant look on his face (such a look as those people always wear who think of nothing but themselves) and asked:

"Surely our poor friend is not in danger?"

Mlle. Bergen replied sadly: "We have not much hope."

"What does the doctor say?"

"Simone won't receive him."

"But we must force her to do so."

Mme. Papillon then collapsed into a chair. Her husband, who had forced a sad expression on to his face, went up to Maurice de Thouars and shook him by the hand, and said:

"Now, tell me all about it."

Concealing, with difficulty, the annoyance which all these visits caused him, Maurice de Thouars replied:

"For some little time the health of our dear Simon has caused us great anxiety."

"She doesn't abuse her health, does she?"

"Alas! yes; but what has knocked everything on the head is the visit of the Phantom!"

On hearing the word "phantom", the Baroness gave a start:

"The Phantom!" she cried, waving her arms in the air; "The Phantom! Ah! don't speak to me about it. It seems to me that I see him ever prowling about me."

"Baroness! Calm yourself! Don't think such things!" said the companion. Then she added: "What about us, we who have actually seen him?"

"If I'd seen him, I should have died," said the Baroness. And she continued: "I have been thinking about going to our Courteuil Castle, which is between Dreux and Mantes."

"It is a wonderful place, isn't it?" declared Mlle. Bergen. "Our poor Simone visited it last summer, and she told me that the Baron had most marvellous art treasures there."

Mme. Papillon continued: "It seems to me that with the shelter of those high, thick walls behind the drawbridge. which we had specially built, we should have felt very safe; but my husband's secretary, Monsieur Luchner, has dissuaded us from going. He said that if the Phantom wished to visit us, he would get in our castle just as easily as in our house in Paris, so I shall stay here. But I'm so upset – I can't get any sleep at all. This awful ghost, I see him everywhere; during the night; during the day. It is dreadful!" she added.

And suddenly shrieking out, she pointed a trembling anger to the door, which had just opened: "Here he is!" she cried. "It is he! It is he!"

"Why, no!" said Elsa Bergen. "It is our footman, Dominique."

"I have just come to remind you that Monsieur Chantecoq has been waiting for you a quarter of an hour," said Dominique.

"Chantecoq!" exclaimed Baroness Papillon. "Chantecoq, the king of the detectives! Oh! show him in! Show him in quickly, I want to see him. I want to place myself under his protection."

"Dominique! Show Monsieur Chantecoq in," ordered Mlle. Bergen.

The footman went out and returned a few minutes later with the celebrated detective. Mlle. Bergen presented him to the Papillons.

Chantecoq bowed to the Baroness, who looked at him with terror in her eyes. Then Chantecoq greeted the Baron and Monsieur de Thouars.

Wishing to break the ice, the companion said: "Baron Papillon is a connoisseur of antiques. He possesses a wonderful collection of curiosities. Amongst his many valuables, he has a beautiful pastel by Boucher, of the Marchioness of Pompadour, and he has a wonderful communion cup from Benvenuto Cellini."

Just at this juncture, Baroness Papillon intervened and said: "Monsieur Chantecoq, you are soon going to arrest the Phantom, aren't you?"

Chantecoq replied with a smile: "I sincerely hope so, Madame!"

"If not, I shall die!" continued Mme. Papillon.

"But I don't see why you should be so frightened of the Phantom – is there any reason why he should attack you any more than anybody else?" said Chantecoq.

"Well; as Mlle. Bergen has just told you, we possess many beautiful things."

"Of course, they certainly would be a temptation for a burglar!"

'You realize that, then!" said Mme. Papillon.

"Be at rest, Baroness. From investigations I have made, Belphegor – for that is the name by which the Phantom is known – appears to be extremely clever; evidence of this is indicated by his attainment of the object which he had in view."

"What was that?"

"The Valois treasure!" said Chantecoq.

"The Valois treasure!" exclaimed Elsa Bergen, Maurice de Thouars and Baron Papillon simultaneously.

"Absolutely," replied Chantecoq.

"Then there was a treasure hidden in the Louvre?' questioned the Baron.

"Yes – under the statue of Belphegor," said Chantecoq.

"And the Phantom stole it?"

"In a very short space of time," replied the detective.

"When was that?"

"Last night."

"Really!" exclaimed Mme. Papillon, "Our Paris police don't seem to be very wide awake."

"Detective Menardier has assured me that he is on the track of the criminal, and that his arrest will only be a question of hours."

"Oh! I can breathe more freely now," said Mme. Papillon.

"Well, I think we may as well be going now," concluded the Baron.

"Yes, I think we may," the Baroness agreed.

"In order to bring you back to your old self," said the Baron, "I think I'll take you to have a cup of tea at Versailles."

"Do please," replied Mme. Papillon.

Then the hare-brained woman added to Mlle. Bergen: "Poor Simone! Please remember us very kindly to her. Let's hope that she'll soon get better. *Au revoir*, Mademoiselle."

After having said good-bye to everyone, the Baron and Baroness departed, and Mlle. Bergen said with a sigh: "Two extraordinary people; she is especially unbearable!"

Chantecoq continued: "I saw that she annoyed you, and I tried to get rid of her."

"And you succeeded, Monsieur Chantecoq! Many thanks!"

"I suppose you invented the story regarding the Valois treasure, didn't you?" declared Maurice de Thouars.

"Not at all!" protested the king of the detectives, "It is absolutely true!"

"Then Detective Menardier told you that he was on the track of the thief?"

"Yes! Menardier thinks that he knows who Belphegor is and that he will capture him. But I am certain that Menardier is on a different track from the one I am following, and that he has made a big mistake. Now you have the reason why I am continuing my investigation of this mystery."

"It is, in fact, an unfathomable business," said Mlle. Bergen gravely.

"That is why," concluded Chantecoq, "I've come to ask Mlle.

Desroches for some information."

"Alas," replied the companion, "she is not well enough even to understand you. However, perhaps I can reply on her behalf – Simone does not have many secrets from me."

"Well. Mademoiselle," continued the great detective, "I shall not hesitate to put an extremely delicate question to you – you are not bound to answer it, but it is of great importance to me."

"Tell me what it is, Monsieur?"

"Were those letters stolen from Mlle. Desroches of such a nature as to compromise the writer?"

Mlle. Bergen thought for a moment, then looking straight into the detective's eyes, she said: "Do you suspect Jacques Bellegarde to be–"

With a brief gesture, Chantecoq stopped her and said: "I have just told you, Mademoiselle, I have no suspicions; I am searching for them."

He continued in a grave tone: "You understand now why I attach so much importance to your reply."

"Monsieur Chantecoq," continued the companion, "don't imagine that for one moment I want to avenge myself on a man who has so cruelly made my poor Simone suffer. I am above such a thing."

Maurice de Thouars approved the words that the companion had uttered by nodding his head.

Mlle. Bergen continued: "Well! To tell the absolute truth, these letters – and Simone made me read every one of them – contained certain passages which would be indeed embarrassing to the person who wrote them."

The companion was just going to continue to speak when Juliette, the chambermaid, rushed into the room and said in a trembling voice:

"Please come quickly! Mademoiselle is worse."

Mlle. Bergen followed the chambermaid to Simone's room.

Maurice de Thouars then got up to follow them, and turning towards Chantecoq, he said: "Will you excuse us, Monsieur?"

"On the contrary, it is for you to excuse me," said Chantecoq. "I was not aware that Mlle. Desroches was so seriously ill."

"She is dying of a broken heart," said Maurice de Thouars, in a grief-stricken voice. Then his eyes flashed with anger and he said spitefully: "This Bellegarde is the cause of it."

De Thouars accompanied Chantecoq as far as the hall, where the footman was waiting to show the detective out, then he rushed up the stairs to the first floor.

When de Thouars arrived in Simone's bedroom, Elsa Bergen, Juliette and a nurse were forcing her to lie down on her bed. She was delirious – her eyes had a scared look in them and her face was distorted. She was waving her arms about in the air and saying:

"The ghost! The ghost! I see it! It is there! It is there!"

With a great effort she managed to get away from those who were trying to hold her down. She rushed towards the window as if she wished to throw herself but of it.

Mlle. Bergen and the nurse ran after her. They successfully caught her and put her in a chair; all her strength had now left her – she was prostrate and her eyes were closed.

After a little while, she revived somewhat, and murmured in a very weak voice, in which there was still a trace of great distress: "Jacques! Jacques!"

Maurice de Thouars said to the chambermaid: "Juliette, go and look for a priest; it is the end – she is dying!"

CHAPTER VII

In accordance with Chantecoq's orders, Jacques Bellegarde remained hidden in the detective's residence. Pierre Gautrais was faithfully guarding him with the aid of the two attack-dogs, Pandore and Vidocq.

A room situated on the first floor had been reserved for the journalist at night but, during the day, it had been decided that he should remain in a little room at the back of the house, the windows of which looked on to the garden. To prevent anyone seeing into the room, they had taken the precaution of lowering the blinds.

Colette had chosen some books from her father's well furnished book-case, which she thought might interest her guest.

After Bellegarde had thanked Colette for the books, she said to him: "I was afraid that you were bored."

"I, bored, Mademoiselle? That is impossible, especially when you are here."

Colette slightly blushed. Then she said without daring to look at him: "Then my company is agreeable to you?"

"More than you can ever imagine."

"You flatter and surprise me," said Colette.

"Surprise; why?"

"Because I am such an ordinary kind of girl."

"Is it that you're so very modest, or are you trying to tease me? I don't wish to pay you a banal compliment," continued Jacques Bellegarde, "but I can only tell you to stand in front of your mirror and you will see from your reflection that you are adorably pretty!"

In a playful tone of voice the young girl replied: "Do you imagine that I never look at myself in the glass, then?"

"Well, if you do, you don't see yourself."

"But I'm not blind."

"Fortunately not, Mademoiselle, or I should have been very discouraged."

"Discouraged?" questioned Colette.

The journalist suddenly looked very sad and ashamed, and said: "Mademoiselle Colette, I don't have the right to answer you."

"Why?"

Bellegarde was quiet. His lips moved, but no sound came from them. Then he sadly shook his head, thereby showing Colette that he wished to keep silent.

Very concerned, Colette asked: "Monsieur Jacques, have I unconsciously caused you any pain?"

"No!" protested the reporter, and incapable of controlling his agonized feelings any longer, he said: "Mademoiselle, let me tell you."

"Do tell me!" said Colette. When Colette said this last sentence she appeared so sweet and so sympathetic that Jacques felt immediately encouraged to confide everything to her. He said, in a voice which was at first hesitating, and which afterwards became gradually firmer:

"Mademoiselle, the first time I saw you, I felt drawn towards you. When I exchanged a few words with you, it seemed to me that you kept yourself very aloof, and it was this aloofness which partly attracted me to you. I wanted to have a long talk with you, but somehow you prevented me from doing so."

"How did I prevent you?"

"By your glance! I grant you that I saw no indignation or anger in it. What I saw was freshness, charm and innocence. I at once guessed that you must be the possessor of a pure and unstained soul."

Then Bellegarde added: "You have never been out of my thoughts from the very first day I saw you."

"Haven't I?" said Colette, slowly lowering her head. For a moment she dared not look Jacques Bellegarde in the face.

Then the journalist continued: "You remember the next day when, just by chance, you saw me with a lady at the Glycines Restaurant, to which incident you have tactfully never alluded?"

"I have forgotten all about it!" said the young girl.

The young reporter paused for a moment, then in a grave voice he continued: "Mademoiselle, what I have to tell you is extremely delicate."

"Tell me! I am not a child, or even a schoolgirl straight from a convent."

"I know that, and I also know that you possess worldly knowledge; that is why I am going to refer to the unfortunate restaurant incident."

"But what good can you do by referring to it?"

"Well! I'm afraid that perhaps you gained a bad impression of me, and I want to get the affair cleared up.

"As you wish to refer to this incident, I'll tell you emphatically, far from laying any blame on you, I pitied you with all my heart."

"I swear to you, Mademoiselle, that this situation was created quite unconsciously by me."

Then Jacques went on to add: "I had only lived for my work until the day I happened to meet the lady you saw at the Restaurant. You won't hear any bad word from me on the subject. To speak ill of her would be an injustice and a cowardly thing to do!" added the reporter.

Colette raised her head in agreement.

"We were certainly never made for each other," declared Bellegarde. And he added with a sickly smile: "You have been able to see that for yourself."

Colette, in repressing a sigh, asked a little timorously: "Still, you have loved her?"

"I thought I loved her," replied the reporter.

Feeling that Colette was not sufficiently convinced, Bellegarde added: "If I had really been in love with her, do you think that I would have broken off the relationship?"

"But she?" murmured the daughter of the detective; "She must still suffer very much."

"She also thought she loved," explained Jacques.

"How do you know?" said Colette, "The jealousy which she has shown regarding you only goes to prove how much she was attached to you. Her love is only a passing fancy – it is not a lasting one, but a fascination, if you will."

"I, myself, was the first to realize our mistake. I agree that it would have been better if we had both realized it at the same time, but I think that later on she did begin to feel that way, because at a recent meeting – the last that we shall ever have – she ended by saying that she thought it would be better if we didn't see each other again."

"It is all very sad," concluded Colette, in a compassionate voice. Then she added: "It must be so terrible if you are truly in love with a person and that person does not reciprocate your love." Jacques was perturbed by these words, and was just going to reply when the door opened noisily and Marie-Jeanne appeared in a very agitated condition. Her hat was tossing about on her head and her face had lost its usual ruddy colour – it was as white as a ghost's.

"Monsieur Jacques," she said, "what do you think the latest rumour is? Everyone wants to say that you are the Phantom of the Louvre!"

And Marie-Jeanne, breathless, collapsed into a chair.

CHAPTER VIII

Colette and Jacques did not appear to be perturbed on hearing the revelations of Madame Gautrais.

When the cook had regained her breath, the journalist said in a kindly voice: "Now, my good woman, tell us what you know."

"Ah! don't speak to me about it, Monsieur Jacques!"

"But I must know what has happened."

"Yes, you are right. Excuse me, Mademoiselle Colette, I don't know what I'm doing; to condemn you, Monsieur Jacques, you, such an honest man! When they saw that my husband wasn't in this affair, they accused you..."

Interrupting, the journalist said: "Come, Marie-Jeanne, explain yourself, please!"

"Well," continued Marie-Jeanne, "as you ordered me, I went to your apartment to get the different things which you required. I was just in the act of getting your pyjamas and socks out of your cupboard when someone knocked three times at the front door. I went into the ante-room and I heard voices calling out:

"'Open, in the name of the Law!'

Then she continued: "What would you have done in my place, Monsieur Jacques? You would have opened it, wouldn't you?"

"Yes! yes! Please continue."

"I opened it and found myself confronted by five men, amongst whom I recognized the little sneak."

"The little sneak?"

"Yes, Inspector Menardier; then one of the men said to me: 'I am the Superintendent of the Police, and I want to speak to Monsieur Jacques Bellegarde.'

"I replied to him that you had gone away; then the little sneak sneeringly said: 'Indeed! I have my doubts.'

"And the Superintendent in a dry tone replied: 'We are going to search his apartment.'

"Before I had even the time to say 'yes', they entered – the Superintendent, the sneak and the three other men. They went straight into your office and, believe me, it didn't take them long to open your drawers and pry into your private papers.

"When they found nothing, the Superintendent started to get impatient; then Menardier drew a letter out of his pocket, and showing it to the Superintendent said: 'It was sent to me today; it is anonymous, but it confirms all my suspicions!'

"The Superintendent then replied: 'But you told me yourself that you saw Bellegarde in the act of pursuing the Phantom!'

"But the little sneak, who did not wish to yield, said: 'He pretended to follow! Sure complicity!'"

And, clasping her fingers together, Marie-Jeanne exclaimed: "I wanted to fight the man, but I did not dare to because I knew he was stronger than I. He turned your book-case upside down, throwing your beautiful books on to the ground. Then he picked up an old exercise book which he perused with interest.

"Meanwhile the Superintendent opened your drawer and brought out a piece of iron."

"A piece of iron?" questioned Bellegarde.

"Yes, I couldn't very well see what it was, but it had the appearance of being very old, He also brought out some letters and some pieces of gold which he put on the desk."

"Some pieces of gold," declared the reporter. "It is a very long time since I had any pieces of gold in my house!"

Marie-Jeanne emphatically replied: "Nonetheless, they were pieces of gold; I'm sure of it.

"Then the Superintendent summoned Menardier, who was still examining the book. As they both showed each other their discoveries, they spoke in a very low voice. I could only hear a few words: 'spell book', 'iron binding', 'Henry III'... and then I thought I heard them speak of a road ... what was it? Ah, I know, Gieri Road.

"Do you know where this road is? I don't. Then the little sneak exclaimed: 'This time I am sure I have our thief.'

"I wanted to question him, but he wouldn't answer me, the old wretch!

"After they had departed with their booty, I waited for about an hour because I was afraid that they might follow me. I then took a taxi and deposited your things at *Le Petit Parisien* offices, and then I got in the taxi again and went as far as Barbes, where I took the Metro;

and here I am."

And Marie-Jeanne concluded: "You see, Monsieur Jacques, that they are going to accuse you of having murdered Sabarat."

Bellegarde replied nervously, and with indignation in his voice: "It's an outrage!"

He then went towards the door, but Colette called him back.

"Where are you going? "she asked in an anxious voice.

"To exonerate myself."

The young girl said in a firm voice: "Remember, my father asked you not to move from here."

The journalist replied: "I cannot live under an accusation such as this."

"Stay, I beg of you."

Eager to confront his accusers, Bellegarde went again towards the door, but, just at that moment, Chantecoq appeared.

On seeing Jacques, the great detective said: "I understand everything. Calm yourself, my friend. Everything will work out all right in the end."

Chantecoq took Bellegarde to one side and spoke to him in a low voice. As the king of the detectives spoke, the face of Bellegarde gradually became more composed, and when he had finished speaking, Jacques said in a satisfied and contented voice:

"Really! Monsieur Chantecoq, you are a genius!".

"Let's just say that I know my business," protested Chantecoq modestly.

And, speaking to his daughter, he added: "All goes well. I think before very long the true Belphegor will be hearing from me."

Chantecoq took Jacques into his laboratory.

He opened a large cupboard in which were all sorts of uniforms. He took out a frock coat, a waistcoat, a pair of black trousers and a sort of Borsalino hat, and gave them to Bellegarde.

Chantecoq then took out of a chest of drawers a wig, a curling moustache, and a beard.

Jacques took off his own clothes and put on those which Chantecoq had just given him,

"We are nearly the same figure," said Chantecoq. "I think they will fit you fairly well."

When Bellegarde had finished changing, the king of the detectives threw a dressing-gown over his shoulders, and after making him sit down, he painted his face a dusky colour so that he looked like an Italian. Chantecoq then fixed on his wig, moustache and beard and gave him a pair of spectacles to put on. "Now! my friend," he said, "just look at yourself in the mirror."

Bellegarde got up and stood in front of the mirror. He was both surprised and satisfied with the result. The transformation was so complete that it was impossible, even for the most critical eye, to denote that he wasn't an Italian – nobody could have recognized the young and already celebrated reporter of *Le Petit Parisien*.

Chantecoq excitedly exclaimed: "It is perfect! A wonderful disguise! I defy anyone to recognize you."

"Your disguise is splendid. I congratulate you," said Colette.

"The merit of my transformation is entirely due to M. Chantecoq," said Jacques.

"Oh! If that is so, I am not surprised," exclaimed Colette. "Papa is a past master in the art of camouflage."

"Anyhow," said the detective, "I have never been an actor."

And, approaching his daughter, he kissed her on the forehead and said: "*Au revoir, cherie!*"

"Are you going out?" said Colette.

"Yes, I'm going with our Monsieur Cantarelli here to keep an appointment with Menardier."

Colette looked anxious, but Chantecoq quickly added: 'Don't be afraid, all will come right in the end."

Colette offered the young reporter her hand, which he clasped fervently.

Then, with a resolute air, Chantecoq said: 'Now, Lord Belphegor, we must be going."

At the same hour, a sports car was on its way from Mantes to Dreux; the Phantom's hunchbacked lackey was steering it, and sitting by his side was the mechanic, who was reading the following note in a loud voice:

"*When you have transported the treasure to the place I have indicated to you, it only remains for you to get rid of Chantecoq, who is becoming a great hindrance.*

BELPHEGOR."

The hunchback raised his head approvingly.

The mechanic then tore the note into a thousand pieces, threw them to the wind, and said: "This detective is a most formidable enemy."

"Possibly!" sneered the hunchback.

And with a grimace in which there was both hatred and cruelty, he added: "But after tonight, he will bother us no more."

PART III

CHAPTER I

Baron Papillon was the only son of a wealthy cocoa merchant, who had left him a vast fortune.

In order to fill in some of his leisure hours, Baron Papillon became an amateur art collector. He knew nothing about the business, but he had the sense to go into partnership with two or three other men – two of them being honest and sincere!

Papillon possessed some really rare and valuable treasures; he was thereby renowned in the world of collectors.

When some influential person granted him the title of Baron – in exchange for a payment by him of the sum of fifty thousand francs, which represented the expenses of obtaining the title – Papillon thought it was time that he indulged in purchasing a castle.

Courteuil Castle was very, very old, and quite a large portion of it was in ruins, including its dungeon and its towers. Papillon chose the castle, in the first place, because it was situated quite near Paris; and secondly, because he could rebuild parts of the historic dwelling, which he bequeathed to the State in exchange for a red ribbon, the possession of which was one of his greatest desires.

The architect he employed was not only an influential member of the Institute, but he was also a remarkable artist. In less than two years he had rebuilt Courteuil so that it appeared as grand-looking as in days of old.

After passing though the great iron gate into the large courtyard, one went through to the Guard Room, which was ornamented with statues and armoury. This led out on to a beautiful stone staircase, at the top of which was a large vestibule, whose walls were hung with wonderful tapestries.

This vestibule was a very beautiful Louis XV room. It contained some lovely pictures too. Leading out of the vestibule was an immense library which contained thousands and thousands of valuable books.

On this day, the man in charge of Baron Papillon's castle was sitting in front of a Louis XIII table on which there was a large box , was covered in canvas and marked with several seals. This person was no other than the mysterious hunchback, one of Belphegor's accomplices. Standing by his side, with his cap in his hand, was the mechanic, another accomplice.

In front of them a concierge in livery was respectfully listening to the hunchback's orders.

The hunchback said to the concierge, in an authoritative voice: "As an unexpected accident has upset the secret working of the dungeons, Baron Papillon has forbidden anyone to visit the castle."

"Very well, Monsieur," replied the concierge, bowing.

The hunchback then told the concierge that the mechanic was a special workman whom he had brought with him from Paris to help with the repairs. He then told him to watch that nobody disturbed them while they were at work.

After the hunchback had dismissed the concierge. there was a silence between the two men. The mechanic was the first to break it, and said:

"Then, Monsieur Luchner, you don't think that we're doing anything risky?"

"I certainly don't," replied the hunchback calmly. And he added: "The Papillons never come here until September."

"But the servants," objected the other.

"They will be away also," said the hunchback.

Taking up a bunch of keys which were on the table, the hunchback made a sign to his assistant to bring the box. The mechanic then carried the box on his back and followed the hunchback.

They went through the dining-room into the drawing. room.

Monsieur Luchner went towards a little door covered with tapestry. The hunchback put his key into the lock and, as the mechanic lifted the box on to his back again, he breathed a sigh of regret. Monsieur Luchner continued: "Let us be satisfied with sharing the Valois treasures with Belphegor."

The hunchback opened the door, and they passed through,

closing it behind them.

The hunchback switched on an electric lamp, and they found themselves at the top of a spiralling staircase. They both descended the steps and reached a corridor at the end of which was a large room surrounded with iron bars. The hunchback told his companion that this was the prison of the castle.

Monsieur Luchner then took a large key from his bunch and placed it in the enormous lock of the prison door. They found themselves in a vaulted room lit by several lamps which were hanging from the walls.

At the end of the room there was an extraordinary-looking fireplace. At one of the sides an electric device was fixed, which had several instruments for measuring gas.

The mechanic put down his box on a massive wooden table and, pointing to the fireplace, the hunchback said:

"That is a high-pressure furnace which I have installed myself."

"Ah! that looks very wonderful to me," said his companion, approaching it.

Baron Papillon's secretary said:

"Supplied by the electric current of the castle, it will give the necessary heat required to melt the Valois gold."

"Decidedly, Monsieur Luchner," said the mechanic.

Pointing to the box, the hunchback said: "We are going to leave this chest here as we were instructed, and as soon as Belphegor rejoins us, we will commence to melt the gold and transform it into bars. Now, we will return quickly to Paris, for we must deal with Monsieur Chantecoq."

Telling Baron Papillon's concierge that they were going to Paris to get something which they needed and that they would return on the morrow, he then slipped a note into the man's hand and said: "That is something for you to drink my health with."

Monsieur Luchner and the mechanic then drove off in their car. Meanwhile the concierge of Courteuil was thinking what a kind man M. Luchner was, despite his hump and bandy legs.

CHAPTER II

Just about this time, Menardier was conferring with M. Ferval, the Chief of the Police Force.

An office boy entered and said that M. Chantecoq had arrived.

"He is exactly on time," said M. Ferval.

"He does not doubt what I am going to tell him," said Menardier.

"Show him in," said the Chief of the Police.

Chantecoq appeared, accompanied by Jacques Bellegarde, or rather Cantarelli.

On seeing this personage, whom they could not possibly recognize as being the brilliant journalist of *Le Petit Parisien*, M. Menardier and M. Ferval showed a little surprise.

Chantecoq immediately said: "My dear Ferval, I want to introduce to you Commander Cantarelli, first numismatist of King Victor Emmanuel II and chief of the Florence Museum – the place which the thief first visited."

Monsieur Ferval courteously saluted the Chief of the Florence Museum, who replied to him with an Italian accent.

Chantecoq shook Ferval by the hand and said: "The Commander is very much interested in this Louvre business, because he is convinced that the thief who visited his museum is none other than our Phantom."

"I think I can soon let you see that the Commander is mistaken," interrupted Menardier.

"I do just want to become convinced," said Cantarelli, with a strong Italian accent.

Ferval and Menardier exchanged a quick glance, and Chantecoq, on seeing it, said: "You can speak in front of M. Cantarelli. I can vouch for his discretion as well as my own."

"In that case, you can know everything," Ferval said. "Thanks to Inspector Menardier's cleverness, the Phantom is at last discovered."

"I haven't actually got him yet," added the little sneak, "but his arrest is imminent."

"Does anyone know his name?" asked Chantecoq.

"Yes, but I ask you both to keep it an absolute secret." said Ferval. "It is Jacques Bellegarde."

"The reporter of the *P.P.?*" exclaimed the great detective in surprise.

As to Bellegarde, he did not move a muscle.

"Yes," said Menardier, affecting a superior air.

Ferval went on: "Certain documents have been found at his house which leave no doubt as to his guilt."

Chantecoq again feigned great astonishment. The false Cantarelli, appearing very interested, continued to listen to Ferval who, pointing to different objects on his desk, said: "Here are some golden crowns which, as you see, bear the stamp of King Henry III."

Chantecoq took one of them, examined it, and passed it on to Cantarelli, saying: "Perhaps Bellegarde intended to start a collection."

"I doubt it," said M. Ferval.

"That is not all," continued the Chief of Police. "Here is an iron binding belonging to a chest which is, my dear Chantecoq, as you cannot help recognizing, exactly identical to the one which you found yourself at the Louvre."

He passed the iron binding to the great detective who, while looking at it very carefully, said: "It is exactly the same."

"But that is not all," said Ferval triumphantly. And, taking up the manuscript which Menardier had found at the bottom of the journalist's bookcase, he added as he showed it to the celebrated detective: "Here is a book of spells, and the contents contained therein throw a light on this mysterious affair."

Chantecoq calmly continued:

"Monsieur Cantarelli, who is an expert in the art of deciphering old manuscripts will, without doubt, be very pleased to look at it."

Bellegarde hastened to add: "I should certainly be very pleased to scrutinize it."

Ferval got up and very politely invited the Commander to sit in his place, and as the latter commenced to turn over the pages of the grimoire. Menardier, who during this time had not ceased to look at Chantecoq with a gloating expression on his face, said:

"Monsieur, will you please excuse me? I must be on

Bellegarde's track without delay."

"Yes, my friend, go quickly."

Menardier saluted Cantarelli, but the latter, being absorbed in the ancient book, had not noticed him. Menardier then shook Chantecoq by the hand, and the latter said, in a slightly joking voice:

"Well, good luck, my friend;" and, pointing a finger at Menardier, Chantecoq added: "Wait a moment!"

"Why?" said Menardier.

"Jacques Bellegarde knows you, and if you do not wish to be recognized, I think you will do well to disguise yourself," said Chantecoq.

Menardier commenced to laugh and said, "You, our leading detective, still believe in camouflage! It was good once upon a time, but now it's finished!"

Chantecoq replied: "You may be wrong."

Ferval accompanied Menardier to the door and whispered a few words to him; Chantecoq and Bellegarde exchanged a furtive smile.

When Menardier had gone, Ferval said to them: "Well, this mystery all seems very clear now, doesn't it?"

The telephone rang. Ferval took off the receiver and listened.

"I will come at once, Monsieur," he said, and as he put the receiver up on the hook, he added: "The Principal wants me."

Chantecoq immediately said: "We will go, then."

"Not at all!" protested the high official cordially. "Here, my dear friend, you are at home. I will come back again in a few minutes." And, after shaking hands with his two guests, he left.

Then the great detective took a chair and sat down at Bellegarde's side.

"All goes well," he murmured; "now, let's get to work!"

Jacques passed Chantecoq the grimoire, on the cover of which, in gothic lettering, was the following;

"SECRET MEMOIRS of COSME RUGGIERI,
astrologer to
HER MAJESTY QUEEN CATHERINE OF MEDICIS."

Chantecoq turned over the leaves of the book, which was written in the French of the period. He stopped at this phrase, which we will translate now in English:

"*Shortly before the days of the Barricades, while His Majesty Henry III assisted at a grand ball in his Louvre Palace, Queen Catherine sent for me.*

"*The Queen was in her private chapel; she was seated near a table on which stood a chest at the corners of which were iron bindings. The cover of the chest bore the Valois Arms.*

"*After bowing before her, I waited until she condescended to speak to me. After a long silence, she said in a grave voice:*

"'*While they dance, the people are revolting against the authority of the Valois, and they are acclaiming our irreconcilable enemy, the Duc de Guise.*

"'*It is no use closing our eyes to the fact. This cursed Balafre wants to seize from my son the crown of his ancestors. He has won the people to his side by fair means or foul.*

"'*Unless the King and I want to fall into his hands, we must leave secretly for Paris without delay, before he realizes his ambition.*'

"*As she pointed out to me the chest lying on the table, she added:* '*Here is the Valois treasure. Before leaving, I want to put it in safety.*'

"*The queen lifted up the lid; the chest contained some golden crowns and precious jewels, amongst which I recognized the diadem which Her Majesty wore on the day of her husband's – Henry II – coronation.*

"*When I had admired these beautiful things, Her Majesty closed the lid again, and turned the secret spring which operated the three locks with which it was provided.*

"*Then she ordered me to follow her.*

"*I carried the chest on my shoulders, bending under its weight. Catherine lit a torch and opened a little door which led to a dark passage through which I followed her. Some minutes after, we arrived in the room of Charles V, and I put my heavy and precious chest in a secret place, beneath a flagstone.*"

Interrupting his reading, Chantecoq said to Bellegarde: "Ferval was right; this document explains everything."

"It certainly does," declared the journalist.

"Let us continue," said the detective, catching sight of the following lines:

"Some days after, the Louvre was invaded by the followers of the Duc de Guise.

"I succeeded in escaping through a subterranean passage, which led on to the great landing in front of the private apartments of King Henry III, and which extended as far as the back of Saint-Germain-Auxerrois's altar.

"I hid for several hours in this church, and when night came..."

"No need to go any further," said Chantecoq. "Through this book, Belphegor has found out about the Valois treasure and also the way to get in and out of the Louvre by means of the subterranean passage, which passage I have suspected the existence of, in spite of historians' and archeologists' advice, but the entrance of which I have never been clever enough to discover."

The reporter exclaimed: "And Belphegor, in order to lay still more suspicions on me, has instructed one of his accomplices to put this document in my house."

"It is as clear as water from a rock," said the great detective; "but what we want to know is how and where our enemy procured this manuscript?"

Chantecoq, who had just taken hold of the grimoire, suddenly smiled furtively. He had just discovered that the first page of the book had adhered to the cover.

Taking a magnifying glass from one of his pockets, he looked at the page closely for a few moments; underneath it, he thought he saw a sort of label on which were some letters faintly to be seen.

"Wait! wait!" he said in a satisfied voice.

Chantecoq took a damp sponge out of a china receptacle which lay on Monsieur Ferval's desk, with which he slightly moistened the edges of the page, and with the aid of a paper-knife, he slowly and carefully separated it from the cover without making the least tear.

A cry of triumph escaped him. On the label was the name of the owner of the book; it was written in gilded letters – and was that of Baron Papillon.

"Look!" said the detective.

The reporter said with astonishment: "Baron Papillon! But still I knew it."

"I also," said Chantecoq.

"He frequents Simone's house."

"It was at Mlle. Desroches's house that I met him; I went there to investigate at her request," said Chantecoq.

Dumbfounded, Bellegarde said: "If it is he, he's rather clever."

"Belphegor?" said the great detective, "No; he is quite incapable of it."

"Well then?"

"It is quite simple. Papillon, who is a collector, or at least thinks he is, has bought this book amongst many others at a curiosity shop and attaches no importance to them. Two things can have happened: he has either resold it, or it has been stolen from him. Now, that is what we want to know," said Chantecoq.

They heard footsteps coming along the passage. Chantecoq put back the *Memoirs of Ruggieri* on the desk, and M. Ferval came into the room.

"Well? Have you read it?"

"Yes, we have read it," replied the detective in a calm voice.

"What do you think of it?"

"I think it is all very confusing," said Chantecoq.

"And you, Commander, what do you think of it?"

"I am of the same opinion as my friend," said the false Cantarelli.

"I suppose, my dear Chantecoq," continued M. Ferval, "that you don't doubt Jacques Bellegarde's guilt any more?"

"H'm!" replied the detective evasively. Then, after a moment or two, he said: "What could be the journalist's motive?"

"I'll tell you," said Ferval. He opened a safe which was behind his desk, from which he took a bundle of letters, and having chosen one of them, he passed it to Chantecoq and said:

"This has been found in his house."

The detective took the letter and read the contents aloud.

"*You are rich and I am poor. I could not commit such a crime.*"

"What's this?" said Chantecoq, showing some surprise. Ferval replied:

"A letter from Bellegarde to Simone Desroches, who was his friend."

"Where has it been found?"

"In Bellegarde's house," said Ferval, at the same time taking back the letter from Chantecoq.

When Ferval wasn't looking, Chantecoq gave a quick expressive glance at the journalist, who understood the meaning of it. This glance clearly signified that he was to keep silent.

In order to conceal the agitated state he was in, Jacques went over to the table and took up the grimoire, and commenced to examine it.

"Did you say that this letter was found in Bellegarde's house?" continued Chantecoq.

"Yes!"

"It's extraordinary."

"Really, Chantecoq, your calculations regarding this affair astonish me."

"Why?"

"Now, you can't trick me, my good Chantecoq."

"But I'm not trying to trick you, my dear Ferval."

"You know as well as I who stole this letter from Mlle. Desroches's house."

"But–"

"You asked Mlle. Bergen, the friend of this young woman, and also Monsieur de Thouars, one of her intimate associates, to keep silent on this subject. You forgot that there were any servants present. Well, Menardier has heard their stories. Although you look on him as a man of little importance, he is far from being a fool."

"And that is how we found out that the Phantom of the Louvre – the mysterious person who Bellegarde has taken as an accomplice – took these letters which I have just shown you and which appear to me to compromise the writer,"

"Will you read that letter to me again," said Chantecoq.

"With pleasure."

The Chief of the Police emphasized each word as he read it:

"You are rich and I am poor. I could not commit such a crime."

Then Ferval added in a firm voice: "Bellegarde has committed this crime."

"Are you sure of it?" replied Chantecoq.

"This letter is sufficient proof."

'Then why hasn't he taken care to destroy it?" said Chantecoq.

"No doubt he was too busy occupying himself in securing a safe place for the Valois treasure."

Chantecoq then said: "Bellegarde's past is above suspicion; he held an enviable position and he had the promise of a brilliant future before him. Well, what do you think his object would be in suddenly becoming an odious criminal? In order to marry Mlle. Desroches? You told me yourself that he had broken off his relationship with her. No doubt you think he has committed this theft so that he can go to the young woman and say: 'Now that I am rich, I have the right to ask you to marry me.'"

"That is so," said Ferval.

"But, my dear man, that doesn't hold water. Could Bellegarde possibly explain to Mlle. Desroches how be came by such a fortune?"

"Well! you see it is all a little complicated," said Ferval.

"Then you really believe he did it?"

"Yes, I'm sure of it," said Ferval; and he added: "As soon as Bellegarde knew of the existence of the Valois treasure, his one object was to get it to an unknown place. So that his whereabouts would not be known, he broke off his relations with this unfortunate young woman, who was really only a plaything to him and whose dowry was nothing in comparison to the millions which he knew he would be able to obtain."

Ferval stopped, thinking that by now he must have convinced his adversary.

But Chantecoq did not appear convinced. He said: "Your reasoning is justified up to a certain point. In any case, you must allow me to point out that Belphegor did a very silly thing in leaving these letters in his house. The iron binding from the chest... the crowns stamped with the effigy of Henry III, and especially these *Memoirs of Ruggieri* which are the key to the secret which he would surely have been careful to keep from the Police."

"But Bellegarde was not an experienced criminal,' said Ferval.

"You mustn't forget that he had an accomplice."

"Oh! no! I haven't forgotten," replied Ferval. "And perhaps I know more about him than you think. Anyhow, I don't see why I should discuss the affair with you. In my opinion, the Phantom of the Louvre can be none other than the thief of the Florence Museum, whom you have been commissioned by the Italian Government to find."

Turning towards Cantarelli who was still pretending to examine the grimoire, he said: "Don't you think that, my dear Commander?"

"Yes, I do," replied the reporter.

"You'll find that all the evidence will fit in," continued Ferval addressing himself to Chantecoq.

"Jacques Bellegarde's profession forced him to visit people of all ranks; he made the acquaintance of the individual in question who told him about the manuscript which was hidden away somewhere – probably in a museum, a library, or some special place. Well, this thief offered him a share in the treasure if he were willing to co-operate in securing it," added Ferval.

"And Bellegarde at once accepted?" questioned Chantecoq.

"It may be that he refused first of all; but who knows? His accomplice may then have put forth all sorts of arguments; he may have offered him hush money. Bellegarde may even have done some things unknown to anyone!"

"Without even the Italian thief's knowledge?" said Chantecoq.

"Why not?" replied Ferval.

"If one wished to give oneself the trouble, one could find out if Louis XVI died at Sainte-Heléne and it Napoleon was guillotined in '93," said Chantecoq in a sarcastic tone of voice.

"Then even now you think that Bellegarde is not guilty!" exclaimed Ferval.

"Would you like to bet with me regarding his innocence?" said Chantecoq.

"Why?" said Ferval raising his shoulders.

"We can then invite Commander Cantarelli to a good lunch."

"Very well, I will," replied Ferval.

Chantecoq then said: "I bet that before eight days have elapsed, I will deliver the true culprits to you."

"I'm afraid you'll lose the bet," said Ferval.

"I shall win," replied Chantecoq.

CHAPTER III

When Chantecoq and Jacques Bellegarde got outside, the first thing the journalist did was to ask Chantecoq if he were satisfied with him.

"Very!" replied the great detective. Then hailing a taxi, he said: "Now let us go to Baron Papillon's house. I have an idea that we shall learn something of interest there."

Some little time later, the taxi drove down the Rue de Varenne and stopped in front of a very beautiful mansion which had been built in the seventeenth century.

At the same time, the hunchback's car was speeding down the road, having followed Chantecoq and Bellegarde. The hunchback was driving it and the mechanic was sitting by his side. The former stopped the car about thirty yards from the hotel.

"Ah!" murmured the hunchback to his companion, "why is Chantecoq visiting the Papillons? Is he looking for me? That would be serious!"

Knowing that he had not been recognized – for Chantecoq and the false Cantarelli had their backs to him – the hunchback steered the car and stopped it immediately behind a large furniture van which was standing outside a neighbouring house.

The door of the mansion opened at last. A morose-looking concierge in grand livery appeared, and in a haughty voice asked Chantecoq what they wanted.

Chantecoq politely replied: "I want to see Baron Papillon."

"Monsieur, the Baron is out," the man drily replied.

"Do you know what time he will return?"

"No!"

"I want to see him with reference to urgent business," said Chantecoq.

With an important and authoritative air, the concierge deigned to say: "You will have to write to M. the Baron and ask for an interview, explaining to him your business."

"We will go at once to the post-office and I will send the Baron a wire. I am certain that he will let me have a favourable and satisfactory reply," said Chantecoq.

They both went away.

The hunchback, who was watching them, waited until they had disappeared round the corner, then he drove his car along to the front of the manse and sounded his horn twice.

Almost immediately the front door opened and the concierge appeared. There was no surly expression on his face this time. The hunchback, still remaining in his seat, called him over to him. The concierge went up to him and saluted, saying: "Good morning, Monsieur Luchner. Have you had a good drive?"

"Yes, very good," replied Belphegor's henchman. Then he said: "What did those people want who have just left?"

The concierge declared: "They wanted to speak to Monsieur the Baron on a serious and urgent business."

The hunchback thought for a moment, and then said: "Is Monsieur in? "

"No, Monsieur Luchner. He is out with Madame Papillon and will not return until very late this evening."

"Good!" Turning to the mechanic, the hunchback said to him in a loud voice: "I shan't need you any more." Then he whispered in his ear: "It is high time to act... tonight then, at eleven o'clock, as arranged."

The mechanic nodded his head in assent and got out of the car.

The hunchback then drove the car into the courtyard of the mansion, put it in the garage, and went into the house.

As we have seen, Monsieur Luchner held an important position in the house. Now, how had he obtained that position? Briefly, it was as follows:

Mathias Luchner, of dubious nationality, was employed as a buyer to a celebrated Parisian antique dealer, and while in his employ he met Baron Papillon.

Owing to the hunchback's great intelligence and remarkable knowledge regarding antiques, Monsieur Papillon offered him a good position as his secretary, or rather his artistic adviser; Papillon was only a bluffer, and hardly knew how to distinguish Louis IV from Louis XVI furniture.

When the hunchback had been in the Baron's service some time, he proved himself so capable that Papillon did nothing without asking his advice first. The hunchback, therefore, knew the Baron's private affairs from beginning to end.

And how had the hunchback – whose past was particularly suspicious – become an accomplice of the mysterious Belphegor? What power had the Phantom of the Louvre over the hunchback?

We must let Chantecoq unravel this enigma.

Luchner, having taken off his black felt hat, sat down in front of a beautiful table. A footman entered with a tray in his hand and said:

"The correspondence of Monsieur Papillon."

Luchner took the letters and examined them carefully. One attracted his attention. After a few seconds' hesitation he decided to open it, and this is what he read:

"*MONSIEUR, THE BARON,*
'*I beg to ask you for an interview. It is with regard to a very serious business which will particularly interest you.*
I remain,
Yours very truly,
     CHANTECOQ, Private Detective."

There was now a sneer on Luchner's face. He tore up the letter in tiny little pieces and put them into his pocket.

The hunchback went quietly into the dining-room, where an excellent dinner awaited him. After dining, he went down to the garage, got his car and drove it out into the courtyard.

Proceeding along the Avenue d'Orleans, he soon reached the gateway of the town. He then drove down the Rue Beaunier and through to an alley in which stood many ramshackle houses. He stopped his car in front of one of these old houses and got out. He took a large key out of his pocket, with which he opened the door. In the front of the house were two windows barred with iron. When he was inside, one could hear the noise of bolts being drawn. What was the hunchback doing in this sinister place?

CHAPTER IV

While Gautrais, together with his two dogs, was keeping guard over Chantecoq's villa, the detective, Colette and Jacques – who had kept on his disguise of Cantarelli – were dining under the veranda.

"It is strange," observed the young girl, "that Baron Papillon has not yet replied. Hadn't you better telephone him?"

"You're in a hurry," replied the detective jokingly.

"I do so want you to capture Belphegor quickly,` replied Colette nervously.

When Chantecoq had gone, Jacques and Colette exchanged a look which said more than words. Love-light was in their eyes.

Colette was the first to break the silence.

"I'm so sorry you're mixed up in this affair; if anything unfortunate should happen to you, I could never console myself."

"Mademoiselle Colette!" exclaimed Jacques, "I really am not worthy of the interest which you take in me."

"But... Monsieur Jacques!"

"Remember, you have only known me a very short time," said Bellegarde.

"I know that you are honourable, loyal and talented, and that you have a great heart, and especially–"

She stopped as if she hesitated to say the words which came from her heart to her lips.

"And especially?" repeated Bellegarde.

"That you will never throw in the towel, whatever the consequences may be," said Colette.

"That is true," said Bellegarde, taking hold of one of her hands.

Then Chantecoq returned, and interrupted their little dialogue.

"No reply from Baron Papillon's house," said the great detective.

"It's extraordinary," said the reporter; "even if he or his wife are not in, there must be servants in the house."

"I will ring again presently," said the detective, sitting down in his seat. "But rest assured, I will find some means of getting hold of him – and with the least possible delay."

Marie-Jeanne entered the room.

"Here are the newspapers." After placing several evening newspapers near Chantecoq, she withdrew.

Chantecoq took one of the newspapers and began to read it.

Bellegarde and Colette also went to take one, but suddenly the great detective said laughingly: "Poor Menardier, he certainly wants to make himself look ridiculous."

Chantecoq showed Bellegarde the page he was reading and pointing out a passage to him, he said: "If you want to amuse yourself, just read this:

"Inspector Menardier has discovered the identity of one of the accomplices of the assassin of the Louvre; he is no other than a young, well-known journalist, and his arrest is imminent."

"Don't you think he's going too far, this detective?" said Chantecoq in an ironic tone of voice.

Jacques did not reply. He continued to read on, then suddenly he looked very serious. Noticing this, the great detective said: "I hope this isn't going to prevent you from sleeping. You don't suppose that Menardier suspects you as Cantarelli, and that he's coming to arrest you in my house? All that is bluff, my dear friend – nothing else."

Without saying a word, Jacques put the newspaper down on the table. He was looking very anxious indeed. While Colette was looking at him, Chantecoq said: "What's the matter, my dear Bellegarde?"

"I don't feel very well, that is all, and I shall be glad if you'll excuse me."

Colette looked at Bellegarde, but he did not return her glance.

Bellegarde said good-night and walked unsteadily into the house.

"Oh! my God," said Colette, growing pale.

"What's the matter?" questioned her father.

The young girl murmured: "If Belphegor has poisoned him..."

"It is impossible," declared the king of the detectives "I

haven't left Bellegarde since this morning. I know he's eaten nothing outside the house, and I don't think you'll accuse Marie-Jeanne of being an accomplice of Belphegor."

"Oh! no, father, but I just wondered if the wicked wretch, unknown to Marie-Jeanne, had succeeded in poisoning our food."

"In that case," replied the great detective, "all three of us would be poisoned."

Colette mechanically took up the newspaper which Jacques had left and commenced to read it. Suddenly she started to tremble and gave a grief-stricken cry. Her father at once took the journal away from her and looked at it to find out what had upset her. A few lines below the passage announcing Jacques's imminent arrest, he saw the following:

"Mlle. Desroches, composer of a poem entitled 'Beautiful Dreams', was taken very seriously ill last night, and there is little hope of her recovery."

Chantecoq looked at his daughter, who, with great difficulty, was trying to keep back the tears, and was saying: "Now I understand! He loves her still!"

Chantecoq affectionately drew his daughter to him.

Suddenly they heard footsteps in the garden, then the barking of the dogs.

"No doubt it's Gautrais taking the dogs for a stroll,' said Chantecoq.

"Father," said Colette. "It's Jacques... he's gone to... to... to find her again."

Chantecoq hurried out to Gautrais, followed by Colette, and he asked him if he'd seen Bellegarde.

"Yes, monsieur, this very instant."

" Well, where is he?"

"He's just gone out. He can't have got very far though."

The detective rushed to the entrance door, opened it and looked outside . Bellegarde had already disappeared.

"Was he still in disguise?" said Chantecoq.

"No," replied Gautrais, "he was wearing his own clothes."

CHAPTER V

Jacques Bellegarde jumped into a taxi and ordered the chauffeur to drive as quickly as possible to Auteuil.

The journalist rang the front door bell of the house with a trembling hand. The news which he had just read had upset his conscience more than his heart.

As he was waiting at the door, Bellegarde was unaware that the mechanic was hiding in the grounds.

The door opened.

"Juliette," exclaimed the journalist, and on seeing her red eyes and mournful face, he said: "What is the news?"

Juliette replied in a very faint voice: "All is finished," and then she burst into tears.

During this time, the mechanic had run over to a little café in the Avenue Mozart, and after some refreshment, he went into the telephone box.

Suddenly Mlle. Bergen appeared. The reporter went towards her.

"Then it's true," said he with trembling lips.

"Our poor Simone died in my arms this afternoon," said the companion.

"As I told you, when I asked you to come and see her again, she was very ill – in, fact she was much worse than we realized."

"Then I am the cause of her death?"

"Certainly your attitude upset our poor Simone deeply, but I think she would have pulled through her illness if only an unforeseen incident had not occurred."

"An unforeseen incident?" repeated Jacques.

The companion went on: "Haven't you heard about the Phantom of the Louvre breaking into the house and stealing the letters you wrote to Simone? Well, this frightened her so much that she grew rapidly worse. Just before she died, she regained consciousness and whispered your name. I asked her if she wanted me to find you, and she said: 'No, he would not believe it and he would refuse to come–'. Then she added in a voice which I shall never, ever forget: 'No; I would rather die with the feeling that he doesn't want me any more – and that I have given him up – that I have sacrificed myself–'.

"Simone's last words to me were: 'You'll tell him that I forgive him–'."

"Poor Simone," murmured Jacques.

The companion sadly shook her head, and said:

"I'm going to let you read her last wishes."

Elsa Bergen went up to Simone's desk, opened, it, and took from one of the drawers a paper which she handed to Jacques. The latter read the following, which had been written by a very shaky hand:

"When I am no more, I wish you to convey me to my studio and lay me on the black divan amongst the flowers which I loved–"

Then the journalist said timidly: "I should like to see her body."

The companion did not answer at first.

"Mademoiselle–" he said, in a beseeching tone of voice.

"Come with me," said Mlle. Bergen.

They both left the boudoir and went into the garden. Reaching the door of the studio, Mlle. Bergen opened it a little nervously. They stood still on the threshold.

The centre of the studio was transformed into a kind of chapel. Simone lay stretched out on the black divan, half buried amongst the roses.

Jacques went up slowly to her body. Death had not taken away her beauty. Her eyes were closed and her face was of an ivory whiteness.

Bellegarde looked down at her. Absorbed in meditation, he gradually knelt down. Mlle. Bergen discreetly left the room.

As the companion was crossing the garden, she saw the footman running towards her.

"Mademoiselle," said he in an agitated voice: "The police are in the house."

"The police?" repeated the companion.

"Yes. Inspector Menardier. He has been ordered to arrest the Phantom of the Louvre. He is accompanied by two other detectives."

"Well, what does he want here?"

"Mademoiselle – he simply asked to speak to you at once. I asked him into the drawing-room."

The companion went into the drawing-room and Menardier, after bidding her good afternoon, said: "We have proof that Jacques Bellegarde is one of the people connected with the assassination of the museum guard, Sabarat, and also with the theft of a treasure hidden in the Louvre."

"Is it possible?" exclaimed Elsa Bergen in great surprise.

"Alas! it is only too true," said Menardier. Then he added: "We have been informed that Jacques Bellegarde has hidden himself in this house."

The companion replied in a sad voice: "Monsieur, someone has died here, and Bellegarde is this very moment at her bedside."

On hearing this, Menardier turned to his men and spoke to them in a low voice.

Jacques was still in the studio, kneeling down at Simone's funerary divan, when suddenly a hand was placed upon his shoulder. He started and turned round – Chantecoq stood before him.

Without taking the least notice of Bellegarde's agitated state, the great detective said to him curtly: "The police are in the house – follow me."

Jacques still continued to look at Simone in a dazed condition, but Chantecoq managed to drag him away. When they were outside, they saw Menardier and the two men, led by the companion, coming out of the brightly-lit drawing-room. They were headed in the direction of the garden, and Bellegarde and Chantecoq only just had time to disappear behind a thicket.

While the policemen, still guided by the companion, were approaching the studio, Chantecoq and Bellegarde crept stealthily to the door which Chantecoq had discovered on his first visit. This door was practically half-open. They went through the portal. Then Chantecoq beckoned to a car which was stationed some yards away, at the side of which Gautrais was standing.

"Get quickly into this car; I will do the rest," said the detective.

When Bellegarde and Gautrais were in the car, Colette drove off.

As soon as they had disappeared, Chantecoq gave a sigh of relief and returned to the garden, reaching the thicket; through the leaves, which he slightly parted, he could see Menardier and his two men standing near the studio, hesitating to enter.

Suddenly Menardier called Elsa Bergen, who was a certain distance away. The companion went up to him. Menardier said a few words to her. No doubt he was asking her to go into the studio with them.

Mlle. Bergen opened the door quite wide and looked in. An exclamation of surprise escaped her, and she beckoned to the detectives.

Menardier gave an angry cry. In the studio there was only the dead body of Simone lying on the black divan.

Turning to the companion, who was just as surprised as he, Menardier said: "Then you lied to me."

"I swear to you, monsieur, that he was here," protested Mlle. Bergen with evident sincerity.

Menardier replied: "Well, he can't be far away; we will search the grounds."

Menardier and his two men commenced a search, and then, suddenly, Chantecoq emerged from behind the thicket and stood before them.

"Chantecoq!" exclaimed the stunned Menardier.

The king of detectives, holding out his hand to Menardier, said: "It is useless, my friend, to upset yourself so – Jacques Bellegarde has already just escaped from me."

Menardier shook his fist, and only just managing to control the anger which was raging within him, he replied: "I thank you, my dear fellow."

CHAPTER VI

On returning to Chantecoq's abode, Bellegarde gave Colette a wringing handshake and sat with his head between his hands.

The detective whispered a few words to his daughter, who immediately tiptoed behind a screen which stood on the left of the door.

Chantecoq approached Jacques, and said to hint in a grave and yet reassuring voice: "Come, my friend, have courage!'

The reporter gave a start and raised his head. At the sight of the great detective his features contorted, and he said in a broken-down voice: "It is terrible, is it not?"

The great detective said to him: "Then you still love this woman?"

"No!" replied Jacques. "I love her no more; in fact, I am quite sure now that I have never loved her."

"Then why this great despair?"

"Because I feel convinced that I am the cause of he death," said Bellegarde.

Chantecoq retorted in a firm voice: "On the contrary, I can assure you that you are in no way responsible for this unfortunate event–"

"Oh! If you could only make me believe that, what a weight you would lift from me – and how grateful I should be to you–"

"Listen to me and do be calm," said Chantecoq.

Sitting down in front of the journalist, the great detective continued: "On my return to the house, I waited in the boudoir, and while there I learnt from the conversation which was taking place in the drawing-room between Mlle. Bergen and several of her friends that Mlle. Desroches was in the habit of taking drugs."

"That's true," said Jacques.

"It may be that she took too strong a dose, following the shock of seeing the Phantom."

"It is quite possible, but it is not certain," said the journalist.

"Granted, my dear friend, but you must admit that my supposition is quite reasonable," replied Chantecoq.

"Yes, I admit that," said Bellegarde.

"Excellent. I haven't finished yet, though. Now, Menardier came to Auteuil at once to arrest you; but, fortunately for you, I was the means of your escape. Well, Menardier placed another supposition before me, namely that Mlle. Desroches's death appears to be most suspicious, and I certainly agree with him. But Menardier suspects you with having poisoned Simone and, of course, I am not in agreement with him on that point."

"But what would be my object in poisoning Simone, and committing such a crime?"

"That is just what I asked Menardier."

"And what did he say?"

"He told me I was talking idly."

"Really," said the journalist, who was very irritated, "Menardier is the worst of brutes."

"No, he isn't," replied Chantecoq. "He's not a genius, but he's no fool. I must say also that he is really quite an excellent fellow."

"Well; why, in spite of all that you have told him about me, does he still persist in suspecting me like this?"

"That's very simple. Menardier is at this moment in the same position as a doctor who, after having made an error in diagnosing a person's complaint, then treats him for a malady which he hasn't got."

"Well, let him sink still further into the mire," said Bellegarde.

"Anyhow, this new accusation which he charges you with can only harm him and benefit us," said Chantecoq.

"But how does it benefit us?" said Bellegarde.

"Daylight is beginning to show. When people find out that you consented to let yourself be charged with all Belphegor's crimes in order to help me in my investigation of the affair, you will be considered a hero. You can write the story of your adventures."

Seizing the detective by the hand, the reporter exclaimed:"Ah! Monsieur Chantecoq, if I had not met you, everything would have gone against me; but for you, I could never have been able to defend myself against such diabolical machinations. If Belphegor, as you believe, poisoned Simone, he must have accomplices in the house."

"That's my opinion, and it is the first thing that I shall go into after I've found out from Baron Papillon the name of the person to whom he sold the grimoire of Ruggieri," said Chantecoq.

"I should think it is impossible to hide anything from you," said Jacques.

With a smile, the great detective continued: 'When people are too timid to speak out what is on their minds, this faculty has been a great help to me."

"Monsieur Chantecoq–" he hesitated.

"Would you like me to speak for you?"

"I will listen," said Bellegarde, comforted by a glimmer of hope.

Chantecoq said: "'Monsieur Chantecoq, I love your daughter.'"

Jacques trembled.

''Have I guessed right?" asked the detective.

"Certainly. Yes; I love Mlle. Colette, and I ask you for her hand, Monsieur Chantecoq."

Chantecoq replied: "I'll tell you, my dear friend, that my daughter also loves you."

"In spite of–" replied Jacques, but he didn't finish.

Chantecoq continued: "When my daughter saw you hurriedly leave the house to go to Simone, she was very troubled, because she was under the impression that you were still attached to her; but now she understands you had only obeyed your conscience – that you were so upset to think you had been the cause of giving her so much pain. Soon, Belphegor will be unmasked, and then the mutual love you have for each other will help you to forget the troublesome times through which you are now passing."

"Monsieur Chantecoq," exclaimed Jacques, whose eyes were filled with tears, "I cannot tell you how happy you've made me feel."

Chantecoq said gravely: "In the meantime, you are going to continue your remarkable impersonation of Cantarelli, under the care of–"

And Chantecoq then broke off, pointed to Colette who had just come out of her hiding-place and was smiling at her beloved. Jacques went to her. "Mademoiselle," said he, "your father will tell you–"

"Nothing," replied Colette. "Because I heard all."

"How?"

"I was there – behind the screen."

CHAPTER VII

Towards midnight, the mechanic dismounted from his motor-cycle in front of the dilapidated house which the hunchback had entered previously. He pulled a knot on a cord which hung across a narrow opening in the middle of the door. The tinkling of a bell was heard inside.

Almost immediately there was the grating sound of iron bolts being moved – the door half-opened and the head of the strange, twisted man named Luchner appeared.

The mechanic went inside and put his motor-cycle up against the wall, the hunchback meanwhile bolting up the door again.

The mechanic found himself in a sort of workshop which was lit by a powerful electric lamp over which was a lamp shade; this was fixed on to bench on which was a gas meter and screws, nippers, etc.

Luchner turned to his companion and said in a sharp voice: "You're very late."

The mechanic replied: "Some very grave things have been happening."

"What?"

"Jacques Bellegarde is still alive."

"What's that you tell me?" rasped the hunchback.

"I tell you, Jacques Bellegarde is alive."

"I don't believe it," replied Luchner.

The mechanic said: "But I'm certain of it."

"Come now, we both saw that he went into the river Oise, and you know as well as I that after five minutes he never reappeared on the surface."

"I can't imagine how it is that he's alive; but as true as I stand here, I saw him only two hours ago entering Simone Desroches's mansion," said the mechanic.

"That is most vexing," said Luchner, convinced at last that his companion was telling the truth.

The mechanic went on: "After I saw him enter the hotel, I ran quickly to a neighbouring café and telephoned the police, informing them that Bellegarde was there. Very shortly afterwards, Inspector

Menardier and two other men arrived in a car; but it was too late, Bellegarde had already escaped."

The hunchback swore angrily and said in a furious voice: "We must find him at once."

"I've already done so," replied the mechanic triumphantly.

"Congratulations! Where?"

The mechanic continued: "After telephoning the police, I hastened back to the house and watched. I was afraid that Bellegarde would leave the house before their arrival, but they got there very quickly. Menardier, or so I thought, had his man in his clutches. I went to get my bike, which I had hidden behind some bushes in the Rue des Lilac, but just as I was about to start off on it, who should I see but Bellegarde jumping into a motor-car standing in front of the little door leading from the Rue des Lilac into the garden, and then I saw our friend Chantecoq signalling to the chauffeur to drive on. When the car had started off, Chantecoq returned to the garden.

"Then I immediately followed the car. Five minutes later, the car drew up in front of Chantecoq's house. Chantecoq's daughter was at the wheel, next to her was Gautrais, the ex-guardian of the Louvre – who Chantecoq has taken into his service – and then I just perceived Bellegarde, who was hidden in the back seat. After that, I made my way here."

"Splendid," said the hunchback.

"Shall I inform the police again that Bellegarde is at Chantecoq's house?"

"No," replied Luchner. And in a sinister voice, he added: "We can do better than that – they will know everything tomorrow night."

The mechanic looked surprised.

Baron Papillon 's secretary continued: "Come and see the little surprise which I am now in the act of contriving." And taking his companion up to the bench, the hunchback picked up a square metal box, at the four corners of which was a little head-screw around which metallic threads, about 16 centimetres in length, were wound, and the four threads were joined together.

The hunchback went on: "This is a bomb of my own invention. It contains explosives capable of destroying a house with as many as six storeys. I experimented with it during the war." And without mentioning to which country he had given his invention, he added: "Thanks to the clock mechanism, the bomb will explode at the exact time I have fixed."

The mechanic said: "But it will be necessary for Chantecoq to be in his house at that time."

"He'll be there," said the hunchback, continuing his work, and after having closed up the gas-meter, he added: "Tomorrow night at ten-o'clock – *boom!*"

"Monsieur Luchner," exclaimed the mechanic "you are a genius!"

* * * * *

The next day, about four o'clock in the afternoon, Chantecoq and Bellegarde – the latter once again disguised as Cantarelli – rang the bell of the Papillon's mansion. "Monsieur Papillon, is he in?"

The concierge replied: "Monsieur and Madame Papillon are both out."

"Indeed!" said the detective, and, taking a letter which he had received that morning out of his briefcase, he gave it to the concierge, saying: "Kindly read this."

The man took the letter and read the following: "*M. Papillon will see M. Chantecoq if he will call on him Thursday at four o'clock.*"

Under the note was a signature which was quite illegible.

The concierge, with a puzzled expression on his face, said: "This is Monsieur Papillon's secretary's writing. No doubt M. Papillon has forgotten the appointment."

Chantecoq commenced to argue, but the concierge shut the door in their faces.

"We will not ring again," Chantecoq said. "I guarantee to you that I will see Baron Papillon tomorrow. I must then get him to tell me from where he obtained the grimoire."

Chantecoq and Bellegarde/Cantarelli returned to Chantecoq's villa. When they arrived at the garden, Chantecoq called out to Gautrais: "Any news?"

"Some employees of the gas company came to change the meter, and as their papers were in order, I let them go down to the cellar with Marie-Jeanne."

"That's quite right," replied Chantecoq.

The detective and the journalist went straight into the office where Colette was perusing the *History of the Louvre*. On seeing them, she arose and went up to them.

"Any news?" she asked.

Chantecoq replied: "No, Baron Papillon was not at home."

Chantecoq went over to his desk, in the centre of which was a letter addressed to him which bore no stamp. He tore open the envelope immediately. It was a card from Baron Papillon, intimating that he unexpectedly had to go out that afternoon on urgent business, and that he would call on him that evening about ten o'clock.

Chantecoq frowned and said to his daughter: "When was this letter delivered?"

"About half an hour ago."

The detective handed the card to Bellegarde to read.

"This is most extraordinary, isn't it?" said the detective.

"It is indeed," replied Bellegarde.

Chantecoq thought for a moment, then he continued: "I'm going to ask Gautrais by whom it was brought."

He went to the window and, opening it, he called out: "Pierre, come to my office immediately."

Just at this moment, Gautrais was letting out the mechanic, who carried the gas-meter which he just replaced on his back, and the hunchback, who had a bag of tools slung over his hump.

As Gautrais was coming back from the door, he heard Chantecoq's call after it had been repeated a second time.

When Gautrais came to the office, the detective said to him: "Who brought this letter?"

"I don't know, Monsieur," replied Gautrais. "I found it under the door."

"Were you in the garden?"

"Yes, Monsieur."

"With the dogs?"

"Yes, Monsieur."

"And how is it that you didn't see anyone and the dogs didn't bark?" said Chantecoq.

"The letter may have been slipped under the door while I was just stretching my legs, or perhaps my back was turned. As to the dogs, they did their work; they growled, and they made me go to the door, otherwise I should not have discovered the envelope on the mat.

"I looked outside the door, but could see no one, then I took the letter and gave it to Marie-Jeanne to put on your desk, Monsieur Chantecoq."

"Oh!" said Chantecoq.

Colette made to question Gautrais, but her father motioned her to keep quiet.

Marie-Jeanne had just come in.

The detective said to her: "Did you accompany the men to the cellar?"

"Yes, Monsieur."

"Did you stay with them.

"Only a moment. I returned on account of my roast beef, which was burning."

Chantecoq frowned. Madame Gautrais continued: "I thought that it was all right to leave them; they seemed to be very nice workmen, and were very polite."

The detective replied in a grave tone: "Yes, *if* they were real workmen."

Marie-Jeanne, feeling that she had committed a grave blunder, lowered her head.

"You, Gautrais, continue your watch; and you, Marie-Jeanne, accompany me, for no doubt I shall have some questions to ask you," said Chantecoq.

"The electricity is on again," declared the cook.

"That doesn't matter," said Chantecoq.

"But what about my beef?"

"It will cook without you."

"But it will cook too much."

"Well, we will eat less."

As Marie-Jeanne passed her husband in the vestibule, she whispered: "The boss doesn't seem very happy, does he?"

"He treats us just as though we were imbeciles," grumbled Gautrais.

A few minutes later, Chantecoq, his daughter, Bellegarde and the cook all went down into the cellar.

The detective turned on the light. He went over to the new meter, against which be put his ear and listened intently. He heard the slow ticking of the alarm clock – he listened again, then turning towards the others he said with his usual *sang-froid*:

"There's a bomb inside the meter!"

"A bomb?" repeated Marie-Jeanne in a frightened voice, and she let herself fall on a case of soap, which collapsed under her weight.

As the reporter helped the cook to get up, Chantecoq said to his daughter: "Run quickly and get Box B for me. It is in Cupboard No. 3 in my laboratory."

The young girl immediately obeyed.

"My God! my God!" lamented Marie-Jeanne, "if it should go off while we are here!"

"Don't talk ridiculously," said Chantecoq. "This bomb will explode at a specified time – some time during the night."

Marie-Jeanne felt a little reassured and continued: "To think that we should be killed during our sleep without even having any warning." Then almost in tears she said: "Monsieur Chantecoq, please forgive my husband and I; I assure you that Pierre was on the watch, and so was I."

"I know that only too well, my good Marie-Jeanne," declared the detective.

"It is so difficult to think of everything. These men were so natural. I'm sure that even you would have taken them for real workmen," she offered.

"You say that there were two of them?" asked the detective.

"Yes, monsieur. A dark, swarthy-looking person in blue overalls with a little black moustache and–"

"Wait! wait!" said Jacques.

"And a hunchback," Marie-Jeanne continued.

"A hunchback!" repeated the journalist.

"He carried his tools in a bag which was slung over his shoulder. The men were very polite and their papers were all in order, or Pierre wouldn't have allowed them to enter," said Marie-Jeanne. "If I had only known, I would have left my beef to stick to the bottom of the oven rather than leave them for a moment."

"And then they would not have been able to trick us," said Chantecoq.

"There's no shadow of doubt," Bellegarde said, "that the two men who brought this meter are the ones who tried to drown me."

Chantecoq then told Marie-Jeanne that he didn't want her any more.

The woman left, and Colette reappeared with the box. It contained many instruments.

Chantecoq put the meter on a table, and with remarkable dexterity he removed the screws which supported the inside.

"You see that I was right," he said, showing his daughter and the journalist the inside of the meter where Luchner had put the bomb and the alarm clock. With astonishing calmness, Chantecoq commenced to remove, with the aid of a pair of pliers, the threads which fastened the clock to the bomb. As he did so, Colette said: "We have had a miraculous escape."

Jacques exclaimed: "All's well that ends well! Now we just have to wait for Baron Papillon's visit."

"Oh, Baron Papillon," said Chantecoq. "I don't think that he'll call to see us tonight."

"Why?" said Jacques and Colette simultaneously.

Chantecoq did not reply to their question, but he said: "Tomorrow, he will have to give me his reason."

CHAPTER VIII

Monsieur Ferval was sitting in his office, reading one of the many reports which were on his table, when his office-boy appeared and said that M. Menardier wanted to speak to him immediately on urgent business.

The Chief of the Police waited impatiently for Menardier, for he brusquely pushed aside his work and told the office-boy to show him in at once.

Menardier appeared; he seemed very agitated.

"I wanted to see you. Without doubt, you're aware of the rumour which is being circulated and which the Press will certainly make a case out of. They say, in fact, many things. For instance, that the death of Mlle. Desroches is most suspicious."

"Yes, I've heard that," declared Menardier: "and from the information which I've gathered on the subject, I certainly think that it *is* suspicious."

"Who, in your opinion, do you think has committed the crime?"

"Bellegarde," replied Menardier, without the least hesitation.

"Again!" exclaimed Ferval.

"Well, hadn't he some motive in getting rid of the unfortunate woman?" said Menardier, "after stealing the letters which are in my possession?"

"Yes, Monsieur Ferval; Mlle. Desroches was likely to become a hindrance to his future plans."

"That is so," said M. Ferval. "I'm going to advise the office of the Public Prosecutor immediately, for it is certain that an autopsy will take place. It is advisable to finish this affair as soon as possible. The public are beginning to get unnerved. Certain newspapers have already published editorials which are not exactly in our favour, and the Montmartre song-writers have written several songs in which they ridicule us. All this is very unpleasant!"

"Monsieur," said Menardier in a sincere voice; "I swear to you that I have done everything in my power to get to the bottom of this affair. I've not had more than four hours' sleep every night."

"My dear Menardier," interrupted Ferval. "I doubt neither your capacity nor your zeal, and I am convinced that your colleagues have also done their best."

"If only Chantecoq had not interfered with my investigations," said Menardier.

"Chantecoq again?"

"Well, monsieur, I assure you, if it hadn't been for Chantecoq, Bellegarde would have been in my hands by now."

"So, it is therefore a duel between the king of detectives and yourself?"

'Absolutely," declared Menardier; then added in an agitated voice: "You've quite unsettled me since you told me that no sooner shall I shadow Chantecoq than he will find out. I feel as though I want to throw in the towel already. If I question him," Menardier continued, "he won't give me a reply; but you are his friend, monsieur. Couldn't you speak to him? You have been friends a long time. I think you would be able to extract the truth from him."

"Very well, I will see him; but I am very sceptical as to the result of the interview."

"I thank you, monsieur. Now that the affair is in your hands, I am at rest."

Menardier was just leaving when an office-boy came in to say that Monsieur Chantecoq wished to see M. Ferval.

"Well; if that isn't strange," said Ferval. "It will be better for the interview to take place here – there will he no witnesses. Meanwhile, you go and call on the police magistrate who is in charge of this affair – it is M. Darely, isn't it?"

"Yes, monsieur," replied Menardier.

"You inform him of the rumours which are being circulated regarding the subject of Mlle. Desroches's death–"

"I understand, monsieur."

Ferval then told Menardier to exit by another door, so that he should not meet Chantecoq. Then turning to the office-boy, who was awaiting his orders, he said: "Show M. Chantecoq in."

The great detective appeared, and the two friends shook hands.

Ferval spoke first: "To what must I owe the pleasure of your visit?'

The king of detectives, with a cordial smile on his face, replied: "My dear man, I want to have a serious talk with you."

"With me?" said the Chief of the Police. "I w as just going to telephone you asking for an appointment – this is quite a coincidence, isn't it?"

"Well, you speak first," said Chantecoq, sitting down in front of his old friend.

"After you," replied Ferval.

"As you please," said the king of detectives; "but I already know what you want to know."

"Sorcerer!"

"Come, my good man, let us put our cards on the table," said Chantecoq with his habitual frankness.

"Although I don't listen through keyholes, I can repeat to you, almost word for word, the conversation you have just had with Menardier. It commenced by him telling you that if it hadn't been for me, he would have already captured Bellegarde."

"That is correct; then you confess–"

"Not only do I confess," continued Chantecoq, "but, in addition, I am going to tell you the reasons why I helped Bellegarde to escape."

"Because you think him innocent," replied Ferval.

"That is one of the reasons, but there is another, special reason." And Chantecoq said in a grave voice: "If Menardier were able to arrest Bellegarde, he would cover himself with ridicule – and that would be his own affair; but you see this ridicule would reflect itself on me, and I don't wish for that."

Ferval replied: "But if you are protecting a culprit, I can't prevent Menardier from doing his duty."

"My old friend, would you believe me if I swore to you that Bellegarde is innocent?"

"Then why doesn't he come forward and prove that the accusations made against him are untrue?" exclaimed Ferval.

"Because I have prevented him from doing so," said Chantecoq. "I want to save you from the unpleasantness of committing a grave error.

"If you want to know all," Chantecoq went on, "let me tell you that if I hadn't crossed Menardier's path, and if I hadn't succeeded in persuading Bellegarde to hide himself, I would not now hold the clue which is going to lead me to the true villain."

"Are you sure?" replied Ferval. "My dear friend, no one admires your genius more than I, but it is possible for even the cleverest of people to make mistakes."

"Then do you think that I have the audacity to think myself infallible?" said Chantecoq.

"I certainly didn't know that you were a modest man."

"Well; I can only inform you that sometimes during the course of my long career, I've committed blunders; but with regard to this affair, I'm certain that I'm on the right track and that you're on the wrong one."

"The future will settle it," replied Ferval.

"Then you still wish to keep on the bet?"

"Yes."

"Very well; but you will have to order the luncheon," said Chantecoq, "and don't forget that Commander Cantarelli is to be invited."

"I won't forget."

"Above all, let us part as the good friends that we've always been," said Chantecoq.

"More so than ever."

CHAPTER IX

In the dining-room of Simone Desroches's mansion, while Juliette was serving them with tea, Elsa Bergen was relating to Mme. Mauroy the last moments of her sister. Suddenly the footman appeared and said: "Monsieur Ferval is here."

The companion arose, a little surprised, while Mme. Mauroy asked her: "What has he come here for?"

"I do not know; but we can't very well dismiss him. If you don't wish to see him, I will talk to him in another room."

"No," said Mme. Mauroy; "I prefer to be here."

Thereupon the companion ordered Dominique to show M. Ferval in.

M. Ferval, after having bowed to Elsa Bergen, looked at Mme. Mauroy who, overwhelmed by her great grief, had remained seated.

The companion whispered to M. Ferval: "It is Mlle. Desroches's sister – she is very upset."

M. Ferval bowed respectfully to Mme. Mauroy, who acknowledged him by a slight inclination of the head. Then turning to Elsa Bergen, he said in a grave voice: "I have come to see you regarding a very painful matter."

Elsa Bergen looked up at him with surprise. As for Mme. Mauroy, she seemed entirely disinterested as to what was happening around her.

"Although the Civil State Doctor has declared the death of Mlle. Simone Desroches to be natural," M. Ferval continued, "we've just become acquainted with certain facts which arouse suspicion."

The companion looked very astonished, and said: "But on the contrary, I can assure you that our poor friend succumbed to heart failure."

"That is not the opinion of the magistrate."

"Do you know what grounds the magistrate has for his conviction?"

"I'm afraid I cannot enlighten you on that point," said Ferval. "All I can tell you is that the office of the Public Prosecutor has ordered that the burial is to be suspended so that a medical examination can take place."

"That is to say, an autopsy–" said the companion.

"Which is to take place with the least delay possible."

At these words, Mme. Mauroy exclaimed in a perturbed voice: "My sister! My sister! Oh! no – not that! not that!"

With much deference, M. Ferval said: "Alas, Madame, the decision of the Public Prosecutor is final."

Mme. Mauroy replied: "Leave her with me just for tonight, monsieur, I beg of you. I have just seen her; she is still so beautiful! Oh! yes, leave her with me until tomorrow."

Very moved by the despair of the lady, M. Ferval said: "Very well, madame, I don't wish to add to your troubles. I will take the necessary steps to prevent the pathologist from commencing his examination until tomorrow morning."

"Thank you so much, monsieur," said Mme. Mauroy; whereupon she collapsed on the couch and burst into sobs.

After M. Ferval had said good-bye, he was shown to the door by Elsa Bergen.

* * * * *

It was about eleven o'clock in the evening, and the house of the late Mlle. Desroches was practically in darkness. The domestics had retired for some time, with the exception of Juliette, who had asked if she might stay with her mistress on the last evening.

Mme. Mauroy, Mlle. Bergen and Maurice de Thouars were gathered around the divan on which the dead body of Simone reposed amongst a swathe of freshly-cut flowers. In a corner of the studio, discreetly standing apart from the others, was the chambermaid, praying.

Noticing that Mme. Mauroy was looking very fatigued, Mlle Bergen said to her: "You really must go and take a little rest."

"Let me stay by her side," replied Simone's sister.

"But you don't want to use up all your strength," said M. de Thouars.

"You may have need of it later on," added the companion.

"That is true," acknowledged the young woman. Then

133

suddenly bursting into tears, she said: "When I think that tomorrow – oh! it is too abominable! Tell me, Monsieur de Thouars, can't you use your influence to prevent the autopsy from taking place?"

"Unfortunately, it isn't in my power to do so."

"My sister! My poor Simone!" continued Mme. Mauroy. "I must embrace you for the last time."

She approached the dead body, and put her lips against its forehead. Then, taking one of the roses from under the body, she slipped it in her corsage and murmured: "I did not realise I loved her so much."

Turning towards Mlle. Bergen, she added: "I can still picture her when she was quite small. I was like a second mother to her – she was eight years younger than I."

She staggered, as if she were going to faint.

In a sweet, but authoritative voice, Mlle. Bergen said: "Don't stay here any longer. You will make yourself quite ill."

"Allow me to accompany you to your room," said M. de Thouars.

Mme. Mauroy took the arm which he had offered her, Juliette came forward saying:

"If madame has need of my services–"

"Yes, go, my child." said Mlle. Bergen to Juliette. "I am going to stay with Simone."

Mme. Mauroy gave a last look towards her sister, then she went out into the garden with M. De Thouars.

Juliette quickly ran to the room which had been reserved for Mme. Mauroy and turned on the electric light. Soon Mme. Mauroy and M. de Thouars appeared on the threshold.

"Monsieur," said Simone's sister, "I cannot tell you how touched I am by your kindness – Mlle. Bergen and you–"

"But it is only natural."

"I shall never forget it," replied Mme. Mauroy.

M. de Thouars respectfully kissed the hand which the young woman held out to him. Then Juliette came forward and said:

"Shall I help you to undress, Madame?"

"No thank you; you go and stay by poor Simone's side."

The girl obeyed. As she was crossing the ante-room, she ran up against M. de Thouars who said to her: "Will you inform Mlle. Bergen that if she gets tired, I will relieve her."

"But, monsieur," observed Juliette, "I will stay there alone."

"You might become frightened, being with a dead body all alone."

"No, monsieur. A good old curate who lived in my native town, once said: 'You are never alone with the dead – their soul is still there.'"

"Ah, well! I am going to take a little rest now," said de Thouars.

M. de Thouars went into the dining-room and sat down in an arm-chair. He looked very sad and tired, and he closed his eyes, hoping that sleep would soon come to him to let him forget his distress for a time.

As Juliette was on her way to the studio, she seemed to hear a rustling of leaves, which was followed by an absolute silence.

She waited a moment – but the silence continued. Feeling nervous, she quickly ran to the studio. As she entered it, she noticed that the lights which were attached to the ceiling appeared to be shining brilliantly. Elsa Bergen was in the act of gathering some roses which had slipped from he divan onto the carpet.

Noticing the troubled expression on the chambermaid's face, Mlle. Bergen said: "What is the matter, Juliette? Is Mme. Mauroy unwell?"

"No, Mademoiselle, it is–"

She stopped as if she dared not go on.

"Come now – speak," said Elsa Bergen.

"Mademoiselle," Juliette then said, "I have just heard a strange noise in the garden. It sounded just as if someone was walking behind the thicket – just where the Phantom disappeared. Oh! if it were that ghost again–"

"Come, my child, don't put such ideas into your head. The Phantom will not come here again. In the first place, M. Chantecoq told us so emphatically; and secondly, the affair is in his hands."

Elsa Bergen had scarcely said these words than all of a sudden the lights were extinguished and the studio was plunged into darkness, except for the guttering light of the candles placed near to Simone.

The two women gave a start – they remained immobile – their eyes were riveted on a little door at the end of the studio which was hidden by a tapestry – it was slowly opening!

A terrified cry escaped them.

The Phantom had just come through the door!

The companion immediately fainted.

Mad with terror, in a voice which was strangling itself in her throat, Juliette vainly tried to call for help. She had not the time. Bounding towards her, Belphegor gave her a terrible blow on the neck with a bludgeon, and the unfortunate girl fell to the ground barely conscious.

Then the Phantom approached Simone's body, snatched it up in his arms, and disappeared with it through the little door by which he had entered.

Juliette, who had not entirely passed out, tried to get up, but she had not the strength to do so, and crawling along on her knees to the door which led to the garden, with a great effort she managed to half open it, and In a distressed voice she called out: "Help! help! help!"

M. de Thouars was just going off to sleep. He got up quickly and rushed into the garden in the direction of the studio.

On seeing him, Juliette, in a weak and terrified voice, stammered out: "The Phantom – has just kidnapped – mademoiselle–"

Maurice de Thouars looked towards the empty divan, on which he could just see the impression which Simone's beautiful corpse had made.

The brave Juliette, at the end of her strength, collapsed.

PART IV

CHAPTER I

About nine o'clock in the morning, Baron Papillon, dressed in a pair of beautiful silk pyjamas, went into his study.

After proudly glancing around the room, which was filled with valuable pictures and most precious art treasures, he went to his desk and, noting that the morning's correspondence had not yet been opened, frowned and immediately rang the bell.

A footman appeared.

In a haughty voice, Baron Papillon said:

"Tell my secretary that I am waiting for him."

"M. Luchner is not here. He left very early this morning," replied the footman. "He ordered me to tell you that he had been called away by M. Barenstein, the great antique dealer, to negotiate a very interesting deal which it was necessary to clinch at once."

"Well, that's all right," declared Papillon, dismissing his servant with a gesture.

Sitting down majestically in front of his desk, he took up one of the letters, and was just about to open it with a paper knife when the telephone rang.

The Baron picked up the receiver and listened. Almost immediately, a horrified expression came over his face.

"Oh, my God! What is that you're saying?" he spluttered.

Just at that moment, Baroness Papillon entered the room in a dressing-gown which looked perfectly ridiculous. Noting the troubled expression on her husband's face, she said:

"Hippolyte, what's the matter?"

With an irritated gesture her husband silenced her.

Then he continued to say over the telephone: "Please accept our heartfelt sympathy, and do not forget to remember us kindly to Mme. Mauroy."

M. Papillon put the telephone receiver on its hook.

Then, turning to his wife, he said in a perturbed voice: "That was Mlle. Bergen."

"The time of the funeral of our poor friend?' said the Baroness.

The amateur art collector replied in a dismal and hollow voice: "The funeral of Mile. Desroches will not take place – at least not just yet."

"Why?"

"Because the Phantom stole her body in the night."

The Phantom!" repeated Mme. Papillon, suddenly becoming terrified. "The Phantom – the Pha–"

She stopped, and incapable of uttering another syllable, collapsed into an arm-chair.

"Calm yourself, my dear Eudoxie, I am here. Now you know that I am a very good shot with a gun! Even yesterday, at the Club House, I made a magnificent shot."

Papillon had boldly lied.

This avowal of courage somewhat calmed the Baroness, and half-opening her eyes, she said: "Hippolyte, tell me what has happened."

"It appears that during the night, while Mlle. Bergen and the chambermaid were watching over the body of this unfortunate young woman, the Phantom appeared. Mlle. Bergen fainted: when she revived, to her great horror she saw that Simone's body had disappeared and that the chambermaid had received a terrible blow on the neck with a bludgeon."

On hearing this, Mme. Papillon became terrified again, and she exclaimed as she put her arms around her husband's neck: "When you think of Chantecoq having the audacity to say that lie would very soon rid us of this ghost! What bluffers these detectives are."

"Give him time," said Baron Papillon.

"I don't want to stay in Paris – I'm too afraid."

"I repeat to you that I am here with you... I do not want to see you in this state any longer. We will leave tomorrow for Courteuil Castle."

The Baroness replied: "No! That isn't far enough away."

"Then where do you want to go?"

"I want to cross the water – to be as far away from the Phantom as possible."

"Very well," said the Baron, coming to the end of his tether. "Where?"

"We will leave for Japan tonight," said the Baroness.

Feeling utterly worn out, the Baron acquiesced: "Very well!"

Whereupon Mme. Papillon got up, and throwing her arms around her husband's neck, she said to him: "Hippolyte, you are a darling."

Baron Papillon was feeling very contented with himself. Suddenly, someone knocked at his door.

"Luchner," said he to himself, "I shall be curious to know whether he had succeeded in clinching this deal or not."

Come in," said the Baron, in a loud voice.

But instead of Luchner coming in, he saw a footman who carried a salver on which was a card; he presented the latter to the Baron.

"Are they waiting for a reply?"

"Yes, Monsieur."

M. Papillon read the message. It was as follows:

"Monsieur, Knowing your great interest in art, I beg to inform you that I possess a most beautiful miniature of Queen Marie Antoinette. It is painted by the well-known artist, Dumont."

"Wait! wait! this is interesting," said Papillon. And he continued to read the remainder of the note, as follows:

"I have made the journey from Holland to France for the sole purpose of seeing you. It is a unique picture, and I would like you to see it before anyone else. Yours truly,
JACOB LEVY-NATHAN, Antiquary at Amsterdam."

With a look of greed in his eyes, M. Papillon declared: "A portrait of Marie Antoinette by Dumont; this is indeed a piece of good luck. They haven't got it even in the Louvre."

Then he told the footman to show the gentleman in.

A few moments later the antiquary was shown into M. Papillon's study. He was an old man of Jewish appearance. A bushy beard hid the lower part of his face, and he had a mass of grey hair on his head. He was scantily clothed in black, and he peered through a pair of large tortoise-shell spectacles which made him look like a sort of modern Shylock; in fact, his appearance inspired one with disgust more than with interest.

But M. Papillon, during the course of his numerous quests for treasures, had seen many another like him. His appearance did not frighten him.

Sitting at his desk in an advantageous position, he invited his visitor to sit down in front of him.

"Let me see this miniature," said Papillon, in a distant voice.

"Monsieur, pardon me, but I haven't it in my possession."

"Then why did you say you had?" said the husband of Eudoxie crossly. "Have you been trying to make fun of me?"

The old Jew, who our readers will already have recognized as Chantecoq, added in a humiliated voice: "It is a subterfuge which I used in order to see you."

Papillon was furious. He got up, and showing him the door, he said: "Get out, or I will very quickly order my servants to run you off."

Standing with his hands joined together, Chantecoq said calmly: "Monsieur, do not be angry with me. I want to put a proposition before you; I swear to you by the God of Abraham, my ancestor, that you will regret it if you send me away."

Papillon said after a little hesitation: "In that case I will listen to you.

"Thank you, monsieur," continued the great detective. "I'm sure that you will be delighted."

"Speak out; my time is precious."

"I know that, monsieur. I will be very brief. I have learnt that you are the possessor of a manuscript of the sixteenth century which bears the title of *Secret Memoirs of Cosme Ruggieri*."

M. Papillon looked surprised and replied: "Indeed! Well; the grimoire has now passed out of my hands."

Jacob Levy-Nathan/Chantecoq, with mouth half-open and

eyes opened wide, listened to the Baron, who said to him: "One of my friends, a member of the Academy of Literature – Monsieur Carpenas by name... do you know him?"

"Who does not know this celebrated Master?" replied the antiquary.

"Well! M. Carpenas, with whom I communicated, informed me that it was of no value whatsoever."

The antiquary raised his head dubiously.

"So I put the grimoire," Baron de Papillon continued, "back into one of the drawers in the Renaissance chest where I found it originally."

"Are you able to give it to me, my dear Master?"

On hearing himself called "My dear Master", Baron Papillon flushed with pride. It was the first time that anyone had called him that.

"I'm afraid it's no longer in my possession. Doubting the authenticity of the chest, I put it up for auction; it fetched quite a good price. So you see the manuscript which I left in one of the drawers has passed into the hands of the buyer."

"Would you be kind enough, my dear Master, to divulge the name of this person?"

"It is Mlle. Simone Desroches," replied Papillon.

Chantecoq gave a slight start, which escaped Papillon's notice, and said: "Mlle. Simone Desroches... Isn't she the young woman who has just died in a mysterious fashion?"

"Absolutely."

Jacob Levy-Nathan/Chantecoq then got up and said: "Well, monsieur, I'm sorry to have troubled you."

"What is the value of this manuscript in your opinion?" Papillon asked.

"It is many years since I have made valuations, but this is a genuine manuscript," said the visitor.

"Then Carpenas must be a fool!" replied Papillon.

"Sometimes even the most shrewd people make mistakes," said Levy-Nathan/Chantecoq.

"Oh! it is too bad," said Papillon, highly irritated. "To think that if it hadn't been for this imbecile, I would still have been in possession of the *Memoirs of Ruggieri*!"

"Ah! Monsieur Levy-Nathan," he went on, "if you are able to obtain the manuscript, I beg you to give me the first offer to buy it back."

"Most certainly, I will, my dear Master," said Chantecoq.

"But," observed the Baron, "I think that it will be very difficult for you – at least, just now – to recover this precious manuscript."

"Why?"

"Because last night the Phantom of the Louvre kidnapped the body of Mlle. Desroches."

"It is not possible!" retorted Chantecoq.

CHAPTER II

Alone in the room which he occupied in Chantecoq's house, Jacques Bellegarde was sitting in an armchair in his ordinary clothes. He was thinking over recent events, when he suddenly got up and began to pace the room.

"Provided Chantecoq has succeeded in getting Baron Papillon to speak!" said Bellegarde to himself. "Then does Papillon know who is now in possession of this manuscript? Perhaps it was stolen from him, and he isn't aware of the fact."

Now, when people are in love it frequently happens that they pass through periods of radiant optimism and most bitter pessimism.

Such was the case with Jacques Bellegarde.

Someone knocked lightly on the door.

"Come in," said Bellegarde.

The door opened and Colette appeared before him.

On seeing her, his depression seemed to suddenly leave him; she was like a ray of light to him.

"Monsieur Jacques," said she in an affectionate, yet reproachful voice, "I'm afraid I must admonish you."

"Really, mademoiselle, and why?"

"Because you have disobeyed."

"I?"

"Yes, my father said you were not to remove your disguise for a single moment."

"That is true," replied Bellegarde.

"Then why have you done so?"

"I had forgotten–" replied the young reporter in an embarrassed tone of voice.

"Are you quite sure?" Colette said, smiling the while. "Now come – tell me the whole truth – have I not the right to know it now that we are engaged to one another?"

"Yes, you have; and forgive me for not having answered you frankly at first," said Bellegarde. "Well, Mademoiselle Colette–"

"Now you may call me just 'Colette'," interrupted the detective's daughter.

"Well, Colette, it annoys me so much to be dressed as Cantarelli; I feel absolutely ridiculous in that disguise."

"Not at all," said Colette.

"You are very kind," replied Bellegarde.

"You know after what happened last night," Colette said, "Menardier cannot fail to have his suspicions."

Then the barking of the dogs was heard, and Colette went to the window and slightly lifted up the curtain.

"Here's my father," she cried. Chantecoq, still dressed as the Amsterdam antiquary, was coming towards the house. "By the look of him," declared the young girl, "I should think he brings good news."

"Let's go to meet him," exclaimed Bellegarde.

"Not before you have put on your disguise," continued Colette.

"Do you command me to do so?"

"I do!"

The two young people then exchanged a loving look, and Jacques went to put on his disguise.

Chantecoq, after removing his own disguise, put on a lounge suit and then went into his study. A few minutes later, Jacques, again disguised as Cantarelli, joined him.

"Have you seen Baron Papillon?" asked Jacques.

The great detective, who seemed to be in an excellent mood, replied: "Yes; and he has related two sensational pieces of news to me."

Very intrigued, the journalist listened intently to the detective, who continued: "The first piece of news is – the manuscript of *The Memoirs of Ruggieri* was once in the Baron's possession, but has since passed into the hands of Mlle. Desroches."

"To Simone?" exclaimed the reporter.

Chantecoq continued: "I conclude that it has been stolen by this unfortunate woman – or by someone in her circle."

"The fact is," said Bellegarde, "she received some very dubious characters at her house."

"Do you suspect Belphegor as being one of her associates?"

The young man thought for a moment, then he said: "I cannot say."

Chantecoq asked him again: "What is your opinion regarding the companion?"

"Mlle. Bergen? I know that she has been in Mlle. Desroches's service a very long time: she always disliked me, but I am quite sure she was very devoted to Simone."

"And this M. de Thouars?" said Chantecoq.

"He was infatuated with Mlle. Desroches; he detested me."

"Is he really the son of a nobleman? Is he unscrupulous?"

"I believe so," said Bellegarde. Then he added: "Do you think that he is Belphegor?"

"No," replied Chantecoq; "so far as I am able to judge him, it seems to me that he is neither intelligent enough, nor audacious enough to play such a rôle.

"Well; now for the second piece of news," said Chantecoq. "Are you ready to hear something really extraordinary?"

"Most certainly," said Bellegarde.

"Belphegor stole the body of Mlle. Desroches last night," said Chantecoq.

"The body of–" murmured Bellegarde, growing pale. "But this is dreadful!"

"On the contrary," said Chantecoq, "it is excellent."

CHAPTER III

The news that the Phantom had stolen the body of Mlle. Desroches soon spread through the neighbourhood, and people naturally became very alarmed. The inquisitive ones assembled together in front of Simone's house.

Two policemen guarded the property's gates; they were forcing back the crowd, which was gradually growing thicker and thicker.

In the studio, in front of the black divan, Mme. Mauroy, Elsa Bergen and Maurice de Thouars were in conference with M. Ferval, M Menardier and the Police Commissioner of the neighbourhood.

The three officials were listening with intense interest to Maurice de Thouars, who was relating the events of the previous night.

The companion was looking very tired and haggard. She still appeared to be very perturbed, and said: "Excuse me if I express myself badly, messieurs, but I am still very upset. What I saw was so frightening."

Ferval – who had decided to preside at the inquest which the magistrate had ordered – replied to her in a kind voice: "Just try to remember exactly what you saw."

"I will do my best," said the companion.

She continued: "I was sitting by poor Simone's side – with the chambermaid – when all of a sudden the electric light was extinguished. There was just the light of the candles, which shone dimly around the room. Then I saw a door slowly opening; this door was situated quite near the divan, and was hidden by a tapestry. Suddenly the Phantom appeared. I lost consciousness. That is all I am able to tell you. Juliette has told us that she wanted to call for help, but the Phantom rushed up to her and gave her a dreadful blow on the neck with a bludgeon. She fell, half dazed, on to the ground; but she says that she is sure she saw the thief take up the body of Mlle. Desroches and disappear with it through the little door."

"Where is this chambermaid?" said M. Ferval.

"She is in bed – still suffering from the violent blow she received."

"Is she in a fit condition to reply to my questions?'

"I think so; in any case, I will take you to see her."

As they were about to leave the room, Menardier, who had just been to look behind the little door, said: "Monsieur Ferval, first of all, may I put some questions to Mlle. Bergen?"

"Certainly."

"Was this door, which leads out on to the garden and is only a few yards away from the boundary wall of the house, locked?"

"It is normally locked," replied the companion without the least hesitation. "However, it is quite possible that it was undone; because I remember that it was through that door that they had to carry the flowers amongst which Mlle. Desroches was lying."

Menardier continued: "Did the Phantom only have to flick a switch in order to extinguish the electricity?"

"Yes, monsieur. This switch, as you have seen, is placed on the left of the door. The Phantom had therefore only to stretch out his arm in order to turn out the lights."

"Which goes to prove," concluded Menardier, "that he knew the house very well indeed."

Ferval and the Commissioner nodded their heads in agreement.

Menardier continued: "Have any of Mlle. Desroches's servants been in her service only a very short time?"

"No, monsieur. The chauffeur has been with us the shortest time of all; he has been here over a year. We had very good references as to his character and he has given us complete satisfaction," replied Mlle. Bergen. "As to the others, they have been in the service of Mlle. Desroches's family for many years. I have therefore been able to know and appreciate them. As I told Monsieur Chantecoq, I can vouch for their characters."

"Then M. Chantecoq has visited here?" asked Menardier.

"Yes, monsieur," replied Mlle. Bergen. "I can even tell you if it interests you–"

"Very much, mademoiselle."

"–that when the Phantom first visited the house, Mlle. Desroches – who had heard of Chantecoq's genius – requested that he should come and investigate; but, as you see, he has been unable to make any discovery."

"And on Chantecoq's very first visit, he declared that the Phantom would never return to Mlle. Desroches's house," added M. de Thouars.

"I must also add," said the companion, "that he then asked us if we would be so kind as not to inform the official police–"

Madame Mauroy, who had kept silent until now, exclaimed: "What a tragedy! If only my poor sister, instead of employing a private detective, had immediately notified the Commissioner of Police, it is more than probable that she would be alive now!"

"Yes, it is," murmured Menardier.

"And now, where is she?" continued Mme. Mauroy. "Oh, Messieurs, you will find her again, won't you?"

Keen to put an end to a scene which was becoming extremely painful, M. Ferval said: "We will now go and see the chambermaid!"

And, addressing Mme. Mauroy: "It will be better for you not to accompany us, madame; you don't want to cause yourself further distress."

"But I want to see and hear everything. I promise you that I'll be brave," replied Mme. Mauroy.

So, guided by Elsa Bergen, they went to Juliette's room, which was situated at the top of the house.

The chambermaid was lying on her bed with her head wrapped up in a bandage.

Mlle. Bergen entered the room first, followed by M. Ferval and Menardier. Mme. Mauroy, M. de Thouars and the Commissioner of Police remained in the corridor; the door of Juliette's room was left open so they were able to hear everything that was said.

Mlle. Bergen approached Juliette and said to her in a kindly voice: "My child, this gentleman is the Chief of the Police; he has come to ask you some questions with reference to last night's incident."

Juliette looked around her in a frightened manner.

"Mademoiselle," said M. Ferval, "will you kindly tell us all that you know?"

"Monsieur," replied the chambermaid, "I was in the studio with Mlle, Bergen when I suddenly saw a door open, and then – and then–"

Menardier was making notes in his notebook. She stopped –

as if the memory of the Phantom had awakened terror within her.

"And then?" said M. Ferval kindly.

"And then," continued Juliette with an effort, "the Phantom appeared. Mlle. Bergen fainted. I cried out. The vile ghost rushed towards me, and gave me a terrible blow on the neck. I fell down, but I did not quite lose consciousness–"

She stopped – she could hardly get her breath. Mlle. Bergen gave her some smelling salts, while M. Menardier whispered to M. Ferval: "This tallies exactly with what the companion told us, therefore–"

With a brief gesture, Ferval silenced him. Juliette had revived, and she continued: "Then, monsieur, I saw the Phantom run towards the divan, take mademoiselle up in his arms and rush away with her."

"I don't want to tire you, mademoiselle," declared M. Ferval, "but I still have one or two questions to ask you."

With a nod of the head, Juliette gave him to understand that she was ready to answer him.

"Did you see the Phantom the first time he entered this house?"

"Yes, monsieur."

"And are you sure that he was the same one as you saw yesterday?"

"Oh, yes, monsieur!"

"Was he clothed in a black shroud?"

"Yes, monsieur."

"And did he wear a black hood over his head which prevented anyone from seeing his features?"

"Yes – and in it there were only two holes for his eyes to peer through. Oh, those eyes! I shall never forget the look in them."

"But you must try to forget," said the high official. And pointing to Menardier, Ferval added: "Here is one of our cleverest detectives, who has promised to arrest the Phantom within twenty-four hours."

"And I won't go back on my promise," added Menardier.

Just at that moment, a taxi stopped on the other side of the road. Two men alighted from it – they were Chantecoq and Cantarelli/Bellegarde. Noticing the huge crowd outside the hotel,

Bellegarde whispered to Chantecoq: "Something must be happening inside."

Chantecoq addressed an old gentleman, who had said that it was no ghost but a vampire; he had been pushed to the back of the crowd by new arrivals. "What is the matter, monsieur?"

In a harsh voice, the old man replied: "A vampire kidnapped a corpse last night."

Back in the mansion's dining-room, Mme, Mauroy, Maurice de Thouars, M Ferval, Menardier and the Commissioner of Police were gathered together.

"The essential thing," said Menardier, "is to get hold of the principal culprit."

"Do you know him? asked Mme. Mauroy.

"Yes, I know him."

"Who is it?"

Menardier was silent. Ferval then motioned to him to continue.

"He who stole Mlle. Desroches's letters," said Menardier.

"Who was that?" said M. de Thouars.

"Jacques Bellegarde."

"Jacques Bellegarde?" repeated Mme. Mauroy, giving the impression that she had never before heard the name.

"Yes," continued the inspector.

But M. de Thouars stopped him and said: "Mme. Mauroy is unaware of the intimate relations which existed between Mlle. Desroches and this journalist."

"Oh, pardon me," said Menardier.

But Mme. Mauroy, turning to Maurice de Thouars, exclaimed: "I want to know everything; you have no right to hide anything from me. Besides, I have guessed. This Bellegarde whom you accuse of having stolen the body of my poor sister... he was... her... her lover?"

"Alas, yes," replied M. de Thouars.

"But what was his object in stealing her body?" asked the young woman.

Menardier did not reply to this question. Realizing that it was only adding to Mme. Mauroy's grief in holding anything back from her, Ferval replied:

"Jacques Bellegarde was the principal instigator of the theft at the Louvre a few days ago."

"Indeed," replied Mme. Mauroy. "Now I come to think of it, I read something in the newspapers just lately about a Louvre ghost, but I did not pay any particular attention to it at the time. Well, how was Simone mixed up in this affair?"

Ferval continued: "As you have learnt, Mlle. Desroches was the paramour of Bellegarde. She was very much attached to him; in fact, she wanted to marry him, but he refused her under the pretext that he hadn't enough money. This was really just an excuse to break with her."

"Which is just what he did," interrupted M. de Thouars angrily.

"And having stolen the Valois treasure," declared Menardier, "he realized that if it became necessary for him to flee abroad, Mlle. Desroches was likely to become a nuisance to him, so he calmly got rid of her."

"The wretch," said Mme. Mauroy, as Elsa Bergen, who had just entered the room, approached her.

"Killed her, how?" asked M. de Thouars.

"By giving her some poison while they were lunching together one day at the Restaurant Glycines," replied Menardier.

"The fact is," said M. de Thouars, "it was just at this time that our poor Simone was taken ill." And turning towards Mlle. Bergen, he added: "Isn't that so, mademoiselle?"

"It is absolutely correct," declared the companion. "I will even add that I had a suspicion of it, but as I had no proof, I said nothing."

"But why, after having killed Simone, would he steal her body?" said Mme. Mauroy.

Ferval replied: "Bellegarde, having learnt that an autopsy was going to be held, and knowing that it would come to light that she had been poisoned, realized that the best thing to do was to get rid of her body."

"It is abominable," exclaimed the young woman. "Oh! Messieurs, you will find her again, you will avenge my poor sister, won't you?"

M. Ferval gravely affirmed: "Justice will be done, I promise you, madame."

As the three detectives went out of the house, some police cyclists, who fortunately happened to pass by the gates, were in the act of helping their two colleagues to push back the crowd which had become thicker and more unruly than ever. At the appearance of the detectives, rumours started to spread. Surely they would hear something now! But in a loud authoritative voice, Ferval said to the policemen: "Send the crowd away; no one at all is to be allowed to enter the house until you receive the order."

The policemen immediately executed their Chief's orders – but not without difficulty.

Ferval went towards his car when suddenly, to his great astonishment, Chantecoq and Commander Cantarelli stood before him.

"And am I included in this order?" asked the great detective of Ferval.

"I'm afraid you are, my dear friend," replied Ferval. "It is a formal order for everybody."

Chantecoq raised his eyebrows; Menardier smiled triumphantly.

Then Ferval continued: "This time, my good Chantecoq, you have lost your bet."

"Do you think so?" said the detective.

"I am certain of it. "There will be some news before tonight," said Menardier, with assurance.

"Yes, I think there will be, too," replied the great detective with a malicious smile.

CHAPTER IV

In Chantecoq's studio, Colette was sitting in front of a typewriter, composing a letter. Suddenly Mme. Gautrais entered the room.

"What is the matter, Marie-Jeanne? My father, M. Jacques—"

"Hush! hush! Mademoiselle," replied the cook immediately. And in a mysterious voice she added: "The little sneak is here."

"The little sneak?" repeated Colette, somewhat troubled.

"Yes, Inspector Menardier," replied Marie-Jeanne. Then she added in a low voice: "He accused my husband of being the Phantom of the Louvre, and came and ransacked M. Bellegarde's flat."

"Well, what does he want?"

"To speak to M. Chantecoq."

"You've told him that my father is not here?"

"Yes, mademoiselle, but he wishes to stay."

"Well, let him wait," replied Colette.

"He wants to speak to you," continued Marie-Jeanne.

"To me?" replied Colette. Then she said: "Show him in," as she tried hard to calm herself.

"Very well, mademoiselle."

Marie-Jeanne returned to the ante-room where Menardier was impatiently waiting with his two colleagues. She made a sign to Menardier to enter the studio. The Inspector went in at once.

"Mademoiselle," said Menardier bowing politely, "your cook has just told me that M. Chantecoq is not in."

"That is correct, monsieur," replied the young girl.

"I am sorry," declared Menardier. "If I am disturbing you, I'll go into the ante-room."

"No, you won't disturb me, monsieur."

As she typed, she glanced at Menardier who was looking towards the window.

She managed to continue typing until the door opened, and Chantecoq appeared with the false Cantarelli in the background.

On seeing Menardier, Chantecoq showed no surprise; Gautrais had warned him of Menardier's arrival, and he said to him in a cordial voice: "Well, Menardier, what can I do for you?" And, turning towards the disguised Jacques, Chantecoq said: "This is my excellent colleague, Menardier, whom you have already met in Monsieur Ferval's office."

Menardier arose and said in a serious tone: "Monsieur Chantecoq, I wish to speak to you privately."

"Splendid," replied the great detective.

Colette left the typewriter and went out, without saying a word, to join Cantarelli.

Chantecoq closed the door again.

Menardier, who had remained standing in front of Chantecoq, looked directly at him and said: "My dear Chantecoq, I've learnt that you are hiding Jacques Bellegarde, the journalist, here."

Chantecoq did not appear at all disturbed by this remark. Quite in control of himself, he replied: "Wait! wait! whoever told you that?"

Menardier replied in a harsh voice: "I know it from a certain source."

Whereupon Chantecoq said simply: "Very well! you may look around, my friend."

"You realize the admiration and the respect which I have for you, Monsieur Chantecoq."

"Then allow me, my dear colleague, to point out to you that at this moment you have scarcely any proof."

"I just want to do my duty," replied Menardier.

"Very well! I say again, you may search as you like."

And, drawing a bunch of keys out of his pocket, Chantecoq said as he gave them to Menardier: "These open all the doors."

Menardier replied: "Monsieur Chantecoq, I don't want the keys; you have only to give me your word of honour that Jacques Bellegarde is not under your roof and I will immediately go away."

Chantecoq glanced towards the window which looked out on to the garden, and seeing Commander Cantarelli sitting there on a seat with Colette, to whom he appeared to be quietly talking, he replied: "My dear Menardier, I give you my word of honour that Jacques Bellegarde is not under my roof."

"Then I will go, and please excuse me for any inconvenience which I have given you," said Menardier.

"I will accompany you to the gate, my friend," declared Chantecoq, who had never shown more cordiality or good humour.

They passed into the ante-room and through to the garden. Colette and the false Commander were talking to Gautrais, who had chained up Pandore and Vidocq because they showed such hostility towards the two detectives who were now standing in front of the entrance door.

Menardier approached Colette and Cantarelli. He bowed to Colette and offered his hand to Cantarelli, who was about to get up and offer his hand when suddenly Menardier seized him by the arm and said: "In the name of the law, I arrest you, Monsieur Jacques Bellegarde."

Colette gave a cry, and Chantecoq angrily said: "M. Cantarelli is my guest, and I forbid you to take him away."

"Shall I unchain the dogs?" asked Pierre Gautrais. Chantecoq silenced him. Then, turning to Menardier, he said: "What right have you?"

Menardier took out of his pocket a letter and presenting it to Chantecoq, said: "Kindly read this."

The great detective read aloud the contents of the note, the writing of which strangely resembled that of the other notes signed by Belphegor. It read as follows;

"I warn you that Commander Cantarelli, who is at this moment in Detective Chantecoq's house, is none other than Jacques Bellegarde."

Instinctively Colette went up to her fiancé, behind whom Menardier's two men were standing.

Then the young reporter, incapable of restraining himself any longer, exclaimed as he took off his make-up: "Yes, it is I – but I am innocent."

Menardier made a sign to his two men, who then stood one on each side of Bellegarde. One of them was going to handcuff him, but Jacques protested and said: "It is quite unnecessary to insult me. I've no wish to run away."

"Splendid," said Chantecoq. And turning to Menardier, Chantecoq said: "Well played, my dear friend, but I must tell you that

155

you have committed the most awful blunder in all your career."

"We will see," replied Menardier, who signalled to his two men to take Bellegarde away.

CHAPTER V

The news of Jacques Bellegarde's arrest spread throughout Paris with amazing rapidity. The first thing Chantecoq made it his business to do was to go to the offices of *Le Petit Parisien* to vindicate Bellegarde's honour.

The whole of *Le Petit Parisien* staff assured him that they would never believe that Bellegarde was guilty of the terrible crimes of which he was accused. Chantecoq said to them: "If I wished I could bring about his release from prison at once; but, if I did so, it would spoil the little game which Bellegarde and I have prepared."

An editor asked: "Then we shall be receiving some fresh news soon?"

"Wait until tomorrow," said the king of detectives; adding: "I promise you, messieurs, that you will be informed before anyone of the arrest of the true Belphegor. Just at the moment, I haven't the right to tell you anything more."

After shaking hands with many of the staff, the great detective went away. As he descended the great staircase, he said to himself: "I'll now go straight home and have a sleep, because I've an idea that I shall have a somewhat busy night."

Let us now return to Mlle. Desroches's mansion. Mme. Mauroy was sitting at a table in the dining-room, deep in thought and looking very sorrowful.

Mlle. Bergen was reading a journal in a distracted manner, when Maurice de Thouars came rushing into the room and said in an agitated voice: "I've good news for you. Jacques Bellegarde has just been arrested at the house of Detective Chantecoq."

"At last," exclaimed Mme. Mauroy, raising her head.

"What a relief," said Mlle. Bergen, adding: "Then has Chantecoq been playing a double game?"

"It may be that he was compromised in this affair," said De Thouars. And he added: "I'm going at once to the Law Courts; I want to find out where this wicked devil has taken Simone's body."

Whereupon Mme. Mauroy told M. de Thouars that she would

go with him.

"Aren't you afraid it will upset you too much?" asked Mlle. Bergen.

"No! no!" said the young woman nervously. "I want to know everything." And with a shaky step, she went out of the room accompanied by M. de Thouars.

Then the footman, who had witnessed this little episode went over to the companion and said: "At last, our poor mademoiselle will be avenged."

"Justice will be done," concluded Mlle. Bergen,

"If he is guillotined, it will be a pleasure for me to see the sight," exclaimed Dominique.

An hour later, an elegant landaulet stopped in front of the iron gate of the Law Courts.

Mme. Mauroy, dressed in deep mourning, and Maurice de Thouars entered the great courtyard.

"The best thing for us to do is to ask to see the Police Magistrate who is in charge of this affair," said de Thouars.

Going up to the officer on duty, he said: "I want the office of M. Judge Darely."

The man showed him the way to Judge Darely's office. After they had climbed the staircase, they arrived in a corridor which was filled with lawyers and journalists who, having learnt of Bellegarde's arrest, had gathered there to get the latest information.

Maurice de Thouars scrawled a few words on one of his cards, which he handed to the man who was keeping guard outside the judge's door.

"Kindly give this to M. Darely at once."

The man took the card and said: "At this moment, monsieur, the judge is cross-examining someone and he has asked me not to disturb him. AS soon as the accused leaves, I will give him your card."

M. de Thouars realized that it was useless to insist, and he went back to Mme. Mauroy and sat down next to her.

Great excitement was going on around them; many lively remarks were exchanged. One journalist said: "I've seen him go by between two detectives – he was handcuffed. When he saw me, he said: 'Tell everyone that a big mistake has been made – I have been wrongly accused, and I assure you that it will not be long before I am free again.' He appeared to be quite calm and self-possessed."

"All the same," said a younger reporter, "they say Bellegarde is charged with some dreadful crimes."

Pointing to Mme. Mauroy, who was still sitting on a seat with M. de Thouars looking very upset and not appearing to take any notice of the conversation which was taking place around her, he went on: "That woman in mourning appears to be very distressed. Do you know who she is?"

Scarcely had he said these words than the door of Judge Darely's office opened. There was immediate silence. Surely they would now hear some news.

Jacques Bellegarde, still looking very calm, appeared on the threshold with the two detectives. On seeing him, Mme. Mauroy sat up with a start, and, before M. de Thouars was able to stop her, she rushed towards Bellegarde and said: "You wretch! what have you done with my poor sister?"

"Madame," protested Jacques, "I have no—"

But before Jacques could finish his sentence, the two detectives hurried him along to the exit.

Mme. Mauroy tried to run after him, but she staggered; M. de Thouars caught her in his arms and managed to sit her down again on the seat, amidst the general commotion.

"She's the sister of Simone Desroches," whispered a law student to M. Troubarot.

About eleven o'clock that evening, an aeroplane landed in a large meadow quite close to the Castle of Courteuil. Two passengers alighted – a man dressed as an aviator and a women dressed in travelling clothes. They both wore leather helmets and masks which entirely hid their faces.

Someone who had been hiding behind a hedge, and who had helped them to land, came towards them. It was M. Luchner, Baron Papillon's hunchbacked secretary.

All three talked for a few moments in a low voice. Then the hunchback showed them a sort of closed shed at the end of the meadow. This shed had previously been used as a nightly resting place for the animals which were put out to graze during the summer.

"We are going to hide our machine here," said he. "And I hope that by tomorrow night all will be finished, and that we shall be able to fly away with the Valois treasure transformed into bars of gold."

The man and woman approved by nodding their heads, and without saying a word, they pushed the aeroplane as far as the shed, the door of which had been previously opened. When they had put the flying machine inside, they went out, and Luchner fastened the door with a very strong chain secured by two enormous padlocks. They then proceeded towards the castle.

However, instead of going through the main entrance, they went along the outside wall until they arrived in front of a little door, which the hunchback opened with a key which he took from one of his pockets.

They went through the door, and some moments later entered the castle through a low window. Then the hunchback whispered to the masked woman:

"Now Belphegor must be satisfied."

The woman said in a grave voice: "Let us hurry! Belphegor is anxious to fly!"

CHAPTER VI

At the same hour, two policemen were standing outside Simone's mansion keeping guard. One of them said to the other as he pointed to the house, which appeared to be in darkness: "I really don't know why they've put us here."

"I think we'd be better off in our beds," replied the other policeman. "Still, orders are orders."

However, had the policemen ventured into the garden of the house, they would have soon learnt that their presence was very much needed. Hidden behind a bush, they would have perceived Belphegor – the Phantom of the Louvre – draped in his black shroud, with his head covered in his strange hood; he appeared to be waiting for something to happen. A faint light shone across the glass door of the vestibule.

Soon this door half-opened, and Elsa Bergen appeared. She looked round to ensure that she had not been followed and went towards the studio; she opened the studio door and went inside. She quickly switched on the electric light.

Without the least hesitation, Mlle. Bergen went towards a Renaissance chest. It was the one which had belonged to Baron Papillon.

The companion moved a secret spring which was hidden behind a hinge; then one of the flaps of the lid slowly opened, and she was just going to put her hand inside the chest, when a slight noise made her turn round.

The Phantom of the Louvre was standing in the studio! The companion was very astonished to see the ghost, but she showed no signs of fear and said simply:

"Whatever are you doing here, Simone?"

The Phantom did not reply, but brusquely tore off its shroud, hood and mask. This time Elsa Bergen shrieked out in terror, for instead of seeing Simone, she saw Chantecoq standing before her.

The companion was so frightened, she dared not move. Chantecoq seized her by the wrists and said to her: "Now then, woman, explain yourself."

The companion closed her eyes and staggered. Chantecoq

supported her and found that she was no more than a rag between his arms.

"Fainted," he thought; "so much the better. When she revives, she'll probably tell me everything."

Then Chantecoq laid her on a couch. As he was trying to resuscitate her, she drew from her corsage a stiletto – the detective did not perceive her action – and plunged it into Chantecoq's breast.

Chantecoq collapsed on to the ground.

The murderess got up and looked triumphantly at him. She then rushed towards the door but, just as she reached it, it suddenly opened and Gautrais, accompanied by Pandore and Vidocq, barred her exit.

Elsa Bergen gave a scream as of a trapped animal. This was followed by a loud roar of laughter from Chantecoq, who said to her: "So you take me for a fool, do you?"

In a second he was on his feet, and went over to Elsa Bergen who looked at him with terror in her eyes. He stopped a few steps away from her and, taking off his waistcoat, showed her a fine coat of mail which entirely covered his chest.

"Now then, confess everything."

The companion sat down in an armchair, and while Gautrais remained on guard by the door with his two dogs, Chantecoq said to her: "Mademoiselle, first of all you will explain to me why, when you saw the Phantom appear, you said: 'Whatever are you doing here, Simone?'."

"I will tell you nothing," replied Elsa Bergen, obstinately.

The detective continued: "I am therefore right in concluding that Mlle. Desroches is not only still alive, but that that it is she who is the nefarious Belphegor."

Elsa Bergen still remained silent, and realizing that, for the moment at least, he could extract nothing from her, he glanced round the room. Noticing the Renaissance chest, he went over to it and opened the lid.

"Ha! ha! very good; so that's it, is it?" exclaimed Chantecoq.

The great detective saw suspended inside of the chest a wax figure, moulded in the likeness of Simone Desroches.

"That is really excellent work," said he. "I should like to have

162

the address of the artist who has executed this veritable masterpiece."

Addressing the terrified companion, he said: "Now I understand everything. With the aid of this wax figure, Belphegor could be in bed and also at the Louvre. Belphegor could be dead and alive at the same time – that wasn't a bad idea, for a female poet."

The king of detectives added: "So my presentiment has come true – the key to the mystery was to be found in this house, after all." Pointing to the wax figure, he said to Elsa Bergen: "Now that I have found the copy, I must ask you what has become of the original."

But the companion did not move her lips.

Chantecoq continued: "Very well then, since you do not wish to speak, there remains only one thing for me to do." And he added in an authoritative voice: "Now then, stand up and follow me. Mind, if you make the least noise, these dogs will at once set upon you – and I don't advise you to let them do that."

Realizing that resistance was useless, Elsa Bergen got up and, without saying a word, she allowed Chantecoq to lead her out of the studio. Gautrais followed behind with his two mastiffs.

They reached the little door which led out on to Lilac Road and through which Chantecoq had previously entered the garden.

A motor-car awaited them, and the detective ordered the companion to get inside.

"Get a taxi and return to the house," said Chantecoq to Gautrais.

"Where are you taking me?" said Elsa Bergen to the great detective.

Chantecoq replied: "I'm taking you to a place which will supply you with bread for the remainder of your days."

Just at this time, a strange incident was taking place at Chantecoq's house. Colette, who had decided not to go to bed until her father returned, was waiting for him in the studio.

All of a sudden the front door bell rang out.

"That's not my father," thought Colette. "He has his key, and if he hadn't he wouldn't ring like that."

Colette rushed over to the window and saw Marie-Jeanne, who had gone to answer the bell. She saw her talk for a moment to a man who was coming up the footpath towards the house.

Colette opened the window and called out.

"What's the matter, Marie-Jeanne?"

"A chauffeur has brought a note from your father."

"Has he given it to you?"

"No, mademoiselle. He tells me that M. Chantecoq ordered him to deliver it to you personally."

"Marie-Jeanne, do you know my father's handwriting?"

"Oh yes, mademoiselle. I would recognize it at once."

"Ask this chauffeur just to show you the envelope, and if it is father's handwriting, let him inside."

Marie-Jeanne went back to the chauffeur, who was still waiting in front of the iron gate, and in a resolute tone of voice, she said: "I suppose you're not fooling me, but in these times one can't be too careful. Now will you just let me see the writing on the envelope?"

"With pleasure," replied the chauffeur.

"Yes, it certainly is his writing." Thereupon she opened the iron gate and said to him: "Follow me."

Marie-Jeanne led the chauffeur to the studio where Colette was waiting.

"Are you Mlle. Chantecoq?" asked the chauffeur – who was none other than Belphegor's mechanic.

"Yes," replied the young girl, looking at the man with mistrust in her eyes.

Colette took the letter which he offered to her and glanced at the address. Yes, Marie-Jeanne was not mistaken – this was her father's handwriting.

She opened the envelope and read the contents of the letter aloud; it was written in a visibly shaky hand:

"MY DEAR CHILD,
I have just met with a very serious motor accident,
Come to me.
        CHANTECOQ."

"Where is my father?" said Colette.

"In the hospital at Mantes," replied the chauffeur.

"Is he badly hurt?"

"A broken leg."

"My God!"

The mechanic, anticipating the questions which the young girl would put to him, continued: "As the Post Office was closed, your father ordered a car from the proprietor where I work, and I was told to come. The car is outside and I can take you to Mantes immediately."

Colette looked the man directly in the face. A suspicion had just crossed her mind. Remembering that her father had gone with Gautrais, she asked herself why he had not made any allusion to him in his note. There was evidently some mystery which needed elucidating, and continuing to look at the man very hard, she said: "My father was not alone. His valet accompanied him. What has become of him?"

The mechanic replied in a rather indolent voice: 'How should I know, mademoiselle? I can't tell you. I'm only doing what I've been told to do." Then he added: "It may be that M. Chantecoq's valet is hurt also. My boss gave me the letter which I've just passed to you, but he told me nothing about it – so I can't tell you anything more."

Colette brusquely exclaimed: "You lie! you lie! My father hasn't written this note at all."

Colette was just going to take the telephone receiver off its hook, when the mechanic produced a revolver from his pocket and, brandishing it in front of her, said: "Hands up, or I'll shoot you."

Marie-Jeanne was terrified, and immediately obeyed. Colette crossed her arms on her chest, saying: "What do you want with me?"

"Now just listen here–" said the mechanic, continuing to threaten the girl with his revolver.

CHAPTER VII

At Courteuil Castle, in an elegant but rather showy dressing-room which belonged to none other than Baroness Papillon, the woman we have previously seen alight from the aeroplane was sitting in front of a dressing table.

Standing near her was her companion, who was still in flying kit, looking at her image in the glass. The reflected countenance was that of Mme. Mauroy. After taking off her helmet and mask, the woman gazed at herself for a moment in the glass—a strange smile lurked on her lips. Her eyes shone with excitement. One would not have recognized her for the same woman.

She slowly commenced to take off her clever make-up and her blonde wig, and turning towards Maurice de Thouars, who was looking admiringly at her, exclaimed in a sarcastic voice: "The charade is ended... I've just about had enough of it." And in a dominating voice in which was a trace of mockery, she said: "Have you nothing to say to me, monsieur. Aren't you even going to congratulate me?"

"I'm sorry, Simone—" said M. de Thouars. "But I still feel rather worried."

"The fact is," continued the young woman, "if I hadn't had more guts than you, the Valois treasure would not have been in our possession today.'

"You are extraordinary."

"Say rather that I'm a genius, beloved," said Simone haughtily.

"Indeed, to have so cleverly devised and carried out a plan such as you've done deserves unlimited admiration. You played the most difficult rôle of Belphegor marvellously, and I trembled lest at any moment Chantecoq should discover you."

Simone shrugged her shoulders disdainfully and said: "The chief factor is that all has gone well. I realize that I've been well supported. Just by luck I happened to discover the precious *Memoirs of Ruggieri* at the bottom of a drawer in the chest which I had bought from that imbecile, Papillon. Then Elsa Bergen thought of the brilliant idea of my disguising myself as a ghost; Luchner, my master forger, wrote the letters supposed to have been written by Belphegor, and the greatest mystery of all – the wax figure representing myself – was also his clever work. This was instrumental in my successfully being able to turn the people's suspicions away from me. Then again, my dear Count; you were also most successful in putting the people of our set off the track. Well, we have played out a good comedy, and I must say that you played your part perfectly."

"I'm so glad to know that you appreciated my services," replied de Thouars.

"You did splendidly," said Simone.

"Of course you know I would have followed you–"

"To the Assize Court," said Simone Desroches.

"To death!" replied de Thouars.

"Didn't you realize that I was only joking?"

"Simone!"

"I feel so happy in having succeeded. Now I can tell you everything."

"Yes, please do," said M. de Thouars, "for up till now I only know what you've been inclined to tell me – that is to say, very little – and I was perfectly content to obey you blindly."

Simone Desroches continued: "You will know everything. My fortune had dwindled to only a few hundred thousand francs – scarcely enough to keep me for a year. I saw the imminent approach of poverty. I wasn't able to earn a great deal of money out of writing poetry. It would have been possible for me to make a wealthy marriage, but my independent nature revolted at the thought of being at the mercy of a man who had probably bought me as one buys an expensive toy.

"Believe me, my beloved, before I discovered the manuscript of Ruggieri, I passed through some dreadfully dark days. But when I read the *Memoirs* of Queen Catherine's famous astrologer, I thought the future a little more agreeable, and I said to myself: 'After all, why shouldn't I take the contents of this spell book seriously?' The tone of these *Memoirs* seemed to be so sincere that I had the immediate impression that they revealed the truth.

"The essential factor was to ascertain if the treasure was still to be found in its hiding place. Before running the risk of a venturesome expedition, I was careful to ensure the success of my plans. As regards Ruggieri, I was not concerned. In fact, at the end of his grimoire, he explained clearly that after the death of Catherine and the assassination of Henry III, the successor, Henry IV, was not desirous to obtain the riches of his ancestor and had allowed them to remain buried under the flagstone, their hiding place.

"Well now, after the Battle of the Barricades, Catherine of the Medicis and Henry III were forced to flee from Paris, and they were never able to return to the capital.

"After I had carefully read all the books and memoirs relative to the history of that period, I noted that there was no mention made of the Valois treasure. Naturally, if it had been discovered, I should have seen it recorded in one of these books. So I therefore concluded that the treasure had not been moved from its hiding-place. Thanks to the details given in the writing of Ruggieri, and to the very complete plan which he had left, I very quickly found the entrance to the secret hiding-place, which was exactly under the pedestal of the statue of a black god named Belphegor. It was a very heavy obstacle, which could only be displaced at night time.

"If the subterranean passage which Ruggieri clearly described were still in existence, nothing would be easier than to visit the Louvre during the night and, between two rows of guardians, to carry out the operation. Elsa Bergen suggested that I send Luchner to do the work, but for reasons which you can guess, I preferred to do it alone."

"Were you afraid that the hunchback would want to take all the profits?" said De Thouars.

"Yes, I was. He is Elsa's brother, and I did not wholly trust him. It was then that Mlle. Bergen suggested to me the idea of the ghost. I accepted it with enthusiasm, and the next night, taking with me the disguise which Elsa had obtained for me, I entered the Saint-Germain-L'Auxerrois church. I can assure you, when I found myself alone in this sanctuary, I felt my heart beat a little louder than usual. I called forth all my courage and dressed myself as a hooded phantom. With the aid of a lamp, and the plan which I had detached from the manuscript, I was successful in discovering the flagstone, which was marked with a *fleur-de-lys* and was behind the high altar.

"In accordance with Ruggieri's instructions, I pressed my finger down on the middle of this flagstone. Nothing moved. I pressed it down harder; it seemed as though the flagstone slightly shifted. I then pressed it down with all my might – it moved slightly; I pushed it gradually along and I discovered a spiral staircase which led to the subterranean passage. After passing a sort of crypt, which afterwards proved to be of service to me, I reached a second staircase which I ascended and I found myself in front of a wall.

"I consulted Ruggieri's plan again and succeeded in discovering the secret entrance to the Louvre; but the mechanism of it was so rusty that I was unable to make it function. I then took advantage of Luchner's good services; he returned with me the next day. The hunchback is really quite a genius. Indeed, in less than an hour he succeeded in opening the door hidden in the wall, and we found ourselves on the central landing of the Victoire de Samothrace.

"Then, alone, I entered the Room of the Barbarous Gods. As I was examining the statue of Belphegor, a custodian appeared and I had to make a hurried exit, with bullets from his revolver singing around my head."

"You commenced work the next day," said De Thouars.

"Yes; and a subordinate of Luchner accompanied us."

"The mechanic?"

"Yes. We learnt that the following night that the chief guardian of the Louvre had obtained the permission of his superiors to stay alone on watch in the Room of the Barbarous Gods. That didn't stop us. I provided myself with a club;" and Simone added in a devilish tone of voice: "And as you know, I didn't fail to make good use of that weapon."

"Yet after that, you had the audacity to visit the Louvre again," said De Thouars.

"Certainly; I entered the Room of the Barbarous Gods alone, and saw Jacques Bellegarde in the act of examining the statue, Belphegor, which was lying on the flagstones. I approached him very quietly, intending to give him the same fate as the guardian, Sabarat."

"Do you mean to say-?" said De Thouars.

"Let me continue," interrupted Simone. "Being intent on his examination, Bellegarde had neither seen nor heard me enter, but scarcely had I lifted my arm to give him a violent blow with my club than a hand was placed on my wrist. It was that of an elderly man – I've learnt since that it was Chantecoq, who came from I know not where and interfered in this unfortunate manner.

"With a brusque movement, I managed to disengage myself and escape. I scaled the staircase of the Victoire de Samothrace four at a time, followed by Bellegarde, who was firing his revolver, but luckily none of the bullets hit me.

"When I arrived on the landing, Bellegarde caught me up and I gave him a terrific blow on the nape of the neck with my club. Bellegarde fell down and I hurried towards the secret door, behind which Luchner and the mechanic were awaiting me."

"Yet still you visited the Louvre again," said De Thouars.

"Yes, thinking that the police would set a trap for me, I thought of a way out."

"So the sleeping-gas was your idea?" said Thouars.

"Yes, and Luchner manufactured it."

Suddenly Simone burst out laughing, and said:"Just supposing that the Papillons should get it into their heads to come here."

De Thouars looked very perturbed at the thought.

Still laughing, Simone Desroches continued: "Rest assured; Luchner has allayed my fears in that respect, and if that delightful couple did happen to come here, we would not be long in acquainting them with the dungeons which the imbecile, Papillon himself, has had rebuilt. In this way, the dungeons would at least be of some use."

Simone coquettishly looked at Maurice de Thouars and said: "And haven't you anything to say to me? Perhaps I've done wrong in telling you all these things, and now you won't have any amorous feelings towards one who isn't afraid of making herself the equal of the greatest criminals of the past and present days.'

"Simone," protested Count Maurice, "I swear to you that on the contrary, I have never adored you as much – and that nothing could ever separate me from you."

"Not if I ordered you to go out of my life?" said Simone.

M. de Thouars grew pale. Then in a hoarse voice, be exclaimed: "No, no, don't ask me to do any such thing. I've already suffered too much, and I couldn't stand any more grief."

"Now, don't complain; your grief has been the means of showing me how much you really loved me," said Simone.

"Yes – blindly – passionately–" affirmed the handsome

Maurice. And in a tender yet reproachful voice, he added: "Ah! if I had but known; if I had only been able to guess."

"I didn't like having to torture you, but at the same time I didn't want to run the risk of losing the treasure. But now that the Valois riches are with us, I shall at last to able to realize a dream which I had planned: to live my life! That is to say, to go far, far away – to see new countries, and with the man I have chosen above everyone, with the man I love, with you – with you–"

Maurice de Thouars was overwhelmed with joy and pressed Simone against his breast, while she, assuming a harmonious intonation in her voice, hypocritically murmured the admirable lines of Baudelaire:

"Think of the sweetness
Of you and I, living together
In the land of our birth."

Their lips met in a long, passionate kiss.

Someone knocked at the door, causing the two lovers to separate.

"Come in," said Simone in an irritated voice.

The face of the hunchback appeared. On seeing him, Mlle. Desroches frowned impatiently and said to him: "What is it you want?"

Luchner smiled like a reptile, and said: "Excuse me if I disturb you, but time is getting short now. You forget that we have not yet succeeded in ridding ourselves of Chantecoq, and so long as he is alive we shall always have the fear that he is on our track."

"That is so," replied the handsome Maurice.

Simone exclaimed in a mystified, yet threatening voice: "Belphegor has not said his last word, and M. Chantecoq will do well not to cross our path – for I have a surprise for him."

De Thouars and Luchner looked up in anticipation.

Then Mlle. Desroches continued: "Since you haven't thought of a means of getting rid of Chantecoq, I have given the matter my attention. In a few hours, the detective's daughter will be in our hands. We will then see if he does not become more friendly–"

The hunchback was going to speak. With a sign of impatience, Simone silenced him. Then she said, in an imperious voice: "Let us go now and rest. At dawn we shall begin to melt the gold."

CHAPTER VIII

Baron Papillon, after the way his wife had behaved, was seriously thinking of obtaining a divorce. A terrible scene had taken place between them.

Returning home about seven o'clock at night, the Baron found the Baroness in the large vestibule surrounded by numerous trunks – a sufficient number to fill a removal van.

The Baroness was giving orders to her servants in a most excited and stupid manner.

"What is the meaning of all this?" questioned the Baron, who wondered to himself if his wife had lost the little reason which she had possessed.

"Aren't we leaving for Japan tomorrow?" said the Baroness.

"Damn it," thought Baron Papillon; he had completely forgotten the rash promise he had made.

The Baroness continued: "I must make some preparations. Don't you realize that we are going on a voyage which will take several months?"

And pointing to the many trunks which surrounded her, she said: "After all, I'm only taking what is absolutely necessary–"

"My darling," declared the Baron, frightened of the storm which would not fail to burst forth, "I want a few words with you."

"Well; speak."

"Not here. Let us go into my study."

"Why?" replied the Baroness.

"Because we don't want the servants to hear."

"Belphegor is arrested?" exclaimed Mme. Papillon.

"No, not yet."

"Then why do you raise my hopes?"

"But I haven't said anything to make you think that, my darling."

"Well, speak out now."

"It is impossible to speak here," repeated the Baron. And leading his wife by the arm, he took her into his study.

The Baron was at a loss as to how to open a conversation

which he knew would be a heated one; the consequences of which he could not foresee.

"Well then, what is it you want to talk to me about? I hope you haven't any bad news to tell me," said Eudoxie.

"Not at all."

"Hippolyte, you're hiding something from me," replied Eudoxie.

And suddenly she exclaimed: "I know everything – you have a mistress!"

"I, a mistress? You are mad!" yelled the Baron.

And giving vent to his wrath, Papillon seized his wife by the throat and said: "One word more – and I will strangle you like a chicken."

Mme. Papillon, without trying to disengage herself, let her head fall on her husband's shoulder and in a weak voice, whimpered: "My idol, my beloved, have pity on your silly darling who adores you, and would be happy to die in your arms."

* * * * *

At an early hour the next day, Baron and Baroness Papillon left by motor car for Courteuil Castle.

Whom would they meet there?

As the Papillons' car sped on its way towards the castle, Luchner the hunchback and Maurice de Thouars were in the building's old prison, making preparations for transforming the Valois treasure into bars of gold.

After opening the chest, Maurice de Thouars put on the table a pile of the golden coins stamped with the effigy of Henry III. Luchner, with the aid of a pair of jewellery pliers, commenced to extract the diamonds and precious stones which were set in the diadem of Catherine of the Medicis.

"Of what value is the treasure?" asked De Thouars of Luchner.

Without hesitation, Papillon's secretary replied: "About fifty million francs; the quantity of gold is comparatively small – the precious stones and diamonds are the more valuable."

"Tell me, will it be very difficult to dispose of them?"

"Rest assured, I have taken all precautions. I have already been in touch with an Amsterdam diamond cutter, and he has promised to sell them for me within six weeks."

And as he continued his delicate work, he added: "Has Mlle. Desroches told you how the profits are to be divided?"

"No, and I haven't liked to broach the subject to her."

"Well; she receives fifty per cent, Mlle. Bergen twenty, myself twenty, and my mechanic gets ten per cent."

"That seems to pan out quite well," replied De Thouars.

"Do you think so?" declared Luchner, looking surprised, and with a sarcastic smile, he added: "What astonishes me – and I don't hide it from you – is that she hasn't given you a portion of the treasure. Would you like me to mention it to Mlle. Desroches?"

"Thank you all the same, but I don't desire any payment for the service that I have rendered Mlle. Desroches," replied De Thouars in a haughty voice.

"I was not aware you were so chivalrous; but anyhow, I should think you will be recompensed in some way or another."

"My dreams are just about to be realized," affirmed De Thouars. "In a few days I am going to marry Mlle. Desroches."

"Accept my congratulations," exclaimed Luchner. "You can't complain – you are the most favoured, and I wish you both good luck."

"I thank you for your wishes, my dear Luchner," said a distant voice.

They looked up and saw Simone Desroches coming towards them. She wore only an elegant negligée.

"I see that you're progressing well," she commented to Luchner. And taking up one of the diamonds which the hunchback had just extracted, she said: "What a beauty! The brilliance of it! I've never seen such a splendid one."

"There are some even more beautiful than that," said Maurice De Thouars. "Look at these rubies and emeralds."

"What a pity I can't keep some of them," said Simone. Then she added: "But it is safer to sell everything – and it's also wiser and more profitable."

And glancing at the whole of the treasure, she said to Luchner: "I don't think your valuation of it is sufficient."

"I'm beginning to think that, too," replied the hunchback. And he muttered between his teeth: "Provided that accursed Chantecoq–"

"Chantecoq!" exclaimed Simone. Then she continued: "I told you yesterday that Belphegor hasn't said his last word yet. Our mechanic has just telephoned from the Mantes Post Office to say that he has succeeded in kidnapping Chantecoq's daughter, and that he and she will be with us in about half an hour from now."

"That is a piece of good business," replied Luchner.

"Even if Chantecoq should be on our track, when he finds that his daughter is in our hands – and he won't be long in finding that out – he will refrain from attacking us, and I will have time to fly away with our treasure and – if need be – his daughter."

"It is simply wonderful," said De Thouars.

The hunchback, after extracting all the stones from the diadem, carefully wrapped them in a piece of silk. Then he put the coins and the diadem on a tray and went over to the high-tension furnace. He opened it and put the tray and its contents inside. After closing the oven, he turned a little copper wheel which put the manometer into action.

On the road from Mantes to Dreux, a closed motor car was speeding along at a great rate.

The mechanic, dressed in his chauffeur's uniform and wearing a pair of dark spectacles, was sitting at the wheel.

After passing several cars, amongst which was the Papillons' limousine – which he had not noticed – he eventually arrived at Courteuil Castle.

Colette was sitting inside the car; she wore no hat, a coat was thrown over her shoulders, and she appeared to be in a deep sleep.

The mechanic drove the car into the courtyard, and the young girl still remained motionless in the back seat.

The mechanic got out of the car, and having made a sign to M. de Thouars not to move and to keep silent, he opened the rear door of the car, and taking a bottle out of his pocket, he took out the stopper and forced the girl to breathe the contents of the bottle.

Almost immediately Colette half-opened her eyes, and her bosom swelled as if she was in a hurry to fill her lungs with the fresh morning air.

Leaning on the arm which the mechanic offered her, she put her foot tentatively to the ground – she seemed dazed and fatigued.

"Kindly follow me, mademoiselle; I am going to take you to your father."

Colette murmured: "My father is no worse than I have been led me to believe, is he?"

"No mademoiselle, and I can assure you that your father's life is by no means in danger."

These words appeared to comfort the young girl.

At that point the butler came forward, and the mechanic was bound to explain the presence of his unknown visitors at the castle. He whispered to him one of those plausible stories which he had cleverly concocted on the spur of the moment.

Maurice de Thouars and Colette then went into the castle, followed by the mechanic.

After ascending the main staircase, they entered the large dining-room where the door was situated, which led out on to the staircase leading to the dungeons.

Maurice de Thouars opened the door and invited Colette to pass through.

They descended the steps and arrived at the old prison.

Colette was astonished to see, through the iron bars, Simone Desroches and the hunchback standing in front of the manometer, watching the oscillations of the pointer.

Maurice de Thouars took Colette by the hand and said: "Come in, mademoiselle, I pray you.'

Thereupon Simone turned round. On seeing her rival, she laughed triumphantly.

Colette attempted to turn back, but on doing so, she knocked up against the mechanic, who was standing in front of the door.

In a jeering voice, Simone said: "Have you come to look for your father? '

"Yes, mademoiselle."

"He is not here," Simone replied. And in a threatening tone of voice, she continued: "And if ever he should come here—"

"Here he is!" said the mechanic, raising his cap and taking off his glasses and false moustache.

"Chantecoq!" exclaimed Simone, with incredulity.

The detective immediately pointed his revolver at her.

Maurice de Thouars and the hunchback remained fixed on the spot with fright.

"This time, Belphegor, I hold you!" said the great detective.

As Maurice de Thouars clenched his fists with rage, and the hunchback slyly approached the table, the great detective said to Simone: "You wished to kidnap my daughter through the medium of one of your accomplices, but I arrived in time to prevent him from doing so. This scoundrel, together with your companion, Elsa Bergen, are at the moment in prison – now, let us settle our accounts."

As white as death and very bewildered, with her back supported by the stone wall, Simone stared at Chantecoq in a strange manner.

The hunchback quietly put out his hand to seize a pair of heavy pliers which lay on the bench, and he was about to throw them with all his might at Chantecoq's head – but Chantecoq, whose eyes seemed to be everywhere at once, did not give him time. He fired a shot from his revolver; the bullet just missed the hunchback.

M. de Thouars tried to go between Chantecoq and Simone, but the detective seized him by the neck and said: "I don't want to injure you like that! Don't deprive me of the pleasure of delivering you intact to my friend, Ferval."

No sooner had Chantecoq said these words than Gautrais, accompanied by Pandore and Vidocq, rushed into the room.

The Police Commissioner and four of his men accompanied them.

"Monsieur," said Chantecoq, pointing to Simone and her two associates, "here is Belphegor and her two accomplices – I give them into your charge."

Two policemen caught hold of the hunchback and M. de Thouars, who made no resistance.

The Commissioner approached Simone, and was going to take hold of her, when the wall against which she leant half-opened and revealed a secret passage, which Luchner had shown her the day before in case she might need it in an emergency.

And as she disappeared through the opening, she exclaimed: "You don't hold me yet though–"

The king of the detectives rushed forward, but he was too late; the wall had closed up again.

As Chantecoq threatened the hunchback with his revolver, he said: "Show me how to open this wall at once, or I'll blow your brains out."

Luchner did not hesitate to obey.

Approaching it, he pressed on a hidden spring situated between two stones and the wall opened immediately.

"Let the dogs loose," ordered Chantecoq of Gautrais, who at once released the mastiffs which he held on a straining leash.

Pandore and Vidocq rushed immediately through the opening and dashed up the narrow staircase, which led to a platform of one of the castle towers.

The dogs arrived there just as Simone was going to let herself fall on to a neighbouring rooftop, through one of whose skylights it would be possible for her to reach the hiding place described by the hunchback.

But Pandore and Vidocq were too quick for her; they threw themselves upon her, and as she tried to free herself, she felt their slavering fangs sink into her flesh.

Simone began to realize that all was lost – either she had to surrender, or she must die. As a last resort, she attempted to reach the battlement, but the dogs' teeth went still deeper into her flesh.

She cried out with pain and rage, and fell down on the flagstones. Pandore was just going to bite out her throat when suddenly a whistle was heard; the two beasts immediately let loose their grasp, and quietly went up to Gautrais who, together with Chantecoq, had now appeared on the scene.

The detective took Simone, who was in a half-fainting condition, into his arms and exclaimed: "Now Belphegor, I do hold you."

CHAPTER IX

While this incident was taking place inside the castle, the limousine belonging to the Papillons stopped in the courtyard.

The butler immediately went up to the Baron and Baroness and, before they had time to get out of the car, he exclaimed excitedly: "Monsieur and madame, some extraordinary things are happening here—"

"What's the matter?" asked the Baron as he alighted from the car.

The butler replied: "The police are here."

Suddenly the Police Commissioner appeared at one of the windows on the first floor, and called out to the butler in a sonorous voice: "Telephone to Mantes Police Station and ask them to send an armoured prison van. The culprits are in our possession."

The Baron and Baroness ascended the main staircase.

Sounds were coming from the dining-room. They went in, and scarcely had they entered than they halted, stupefied.

The four policemen were surrounding Maurice de Thouars and the hunchback, Luchner; Chantecoq and Gautrais stood by Simone Desroches, who was sitting on a chair looking at Colette with an expression of hatred on her face. Colette had tactfully sat down in a dark corner of the dining-room.

The great detective advanced towards the Baron and Baroness.

"Madame," he said, bowing, "I promised that I would deliver Belphegor to you."

And pointing to Simone, he added: 'Here he is—"

The Baron, thinking he was dreaming, opened his eyes wide – he could not understand.

Eudoxie stared and stared with astonishment until Simone said in a cynical voice: "Yes. It is I. Don't you know me?"

This was too much for the poor woman. She gave a loud scream and fainted in her husband's arms, who hurriedly carried her into a neighbouring room.

Simone then told Chantecoq why she had committed such crimes, and she added: "You must be content, as you have proved the stronger!"

The king of the detectives looked at her with a sad expression on his lace, and asked: "What has brought you to this?"

She trembled and closed her eyes and said in a weak voice: "Drugs – and then the fear of poverty."

They all silently looked at Simone, who seemed to recover possession of herself; then suddenly she drew something out of her corsage and put it to her lips.

Chantecoq rushed forward – he was too late.

Mlle. Desroches collapsed onto the ground.

The detective and the Commissioner leant over her. Chantecoq opened one of her hands and found an empty glass phial.

"Cyanide; she has expiated her crime."

Maurice de Thouars was immediately stricken with grief.

Everyone bared their heads.

A few minutes later, in the telegraphic room of *Le Petit Parisien*, a wireless operator listened to a communication which he repeated through a speaking tube to an editor who, seated at a table and surrounded by several of his colleagues, took down in shorthand the message, which he then read out to them. It ran as follows:

"Chantecoq, the king of detectives, has just arrested the Phantom of the Louvre – who is none other than a woman – in a castle in the neighbourhood of Mantes."

Suddenly a voice said: "So you see, it wasn't me after all." The voice was that of Jacques Bellegarde, who had just been set at liberty. All his colleagues immediately gathered round him and offered their congratulations.

One of them exclaimed: "What a wonderful story you can give us."

"I have indeed had a most intriguing and romantic adventure," declared Bellegarde.

"Without doubt it, will end in marriage," replied on of his colleagues.

"Perhaps," said Jacques, with a charming smile.

EPILOGUE

A few days later at the Eiffel Tower Restaurant, Chantecoq gave a little luncheon to celebrate the engagement of his daughter to Jacques Bellegarde. Ferval and Menardier were the invited guests.

"Well, my dear Menardier, it seems the old methods are sometimes satisfactory – it isn't always useless to disguise oneself, is it?" said Chantecoq.

'You are master of us all, Monsieur Chantecoq."

Then Ferval stood up with his glass of champagne In his hand and exclaimed: "I drink to the health and good fortune of the engaged couple, and to Chantecoq, the best of friends and the cleverest and bravest of men."

They clinked glasses.

Then Menardier and Ferval made their departure.

Jacques and Colette went over to the window and looked out with admiration on the panorama of Paris.

Suddenly it seemed to them that far, far away, above the Louvre Palace, appeared a sort of black ghost who, after hovering in the clouds for a moment, evaporated into space. Colette instinctively leant towards her fiancé, who gave her a loving kiss. Chantecoq, observing them with a kindly smile, murmured: "Now I'm sure that Belphegor, the Phantom of the Louvre, will never come to life again."